Suspicions at Sunset

(A Bess Bullock Retirement Home Mystery)

by

Allen B. Boyer

Copyright 2015 by Allen B. Boyer

For information, email **Cozy Cat Press**, cozycatpress@aol.com or visit our website at: www.cozycatpress.com

COZY CAT
PRESS

ISBN: 978-1-939816-70-2

Printed in the United States of America

Cover design by Keri Knutson
http://alchemybookcover.blogspot.com

1 2 3 4 5 6 7 8 9 10

For Joan Boyer, the best mother and lover of good books.

Dear Alma,

I hope you are well. Please convey this message to Flo, who said she doesn't have time for letters, and to Rose, who said her eyesight is too poor to read my handwriting. While I miss playing bridge with all of you, I have enjoyed my train trip. The weather in California is still warm and the trees are still full and green, a welcome change of pace from the early fall weather back home. We enjoyed seeing family and sharing some tears, but the time has come for us to return. The train ride back to Pennsylvania will take three days. I will have many stories to share with you when I return. Looking forward to playing bridge with all of you.

Love,

Bess

Chapter 1: MISTER BUTTONS

Seated with her daughter and granddaughter, Bess Bullock was enjoying the experience of traveling cross-country on an eastbound train. For someone accustomed to life in the quiet confines of a retirement home, this unexpected trip to California and back had taken Bess out of her comfort zone. However, she was finding the excursion to be a welcome change of pace from her normal routine of medical appointments, bingo, and working in her gardens.

It was the first time in her eighty-two years that she'd seen the country from the perspective of a train. She found the experience mesmerizing. On the way out to California, she spent a good amount of time looking out the windows at the scenery shooting by. She found it hard to take her eyes off the natural beauty of the land.

Besides enjoying the view, Bess found other ways to occupy her time. Occasionally, she'd fill out a few postcards to her friends back at the Honey Hills Retirement Center. In between postcards and the views, Bess also found her eyes drifting over to Nicole, her young granddaughter.

Nicole, who sat directly across from Bess, was clearly mesmerized by the landscape outside her window. Most of the time, Nicole sat up on her knees with her small face nearly pressed against the glass, looking as though she were trying to sniff the scenery. Sitting next to Nicole, was Bess's daughter, Samantha. From time to time, Samantha whispered into Nicole's ear, and what she said caused both mother and daughter to smile. Watching them enjoy the train ride caused Bess to grin more than once. In Bess's eyes, the beauty of family was more attractive than any landscape outside her window.

On this particular morning, Bess was working on writing out postcards that she'd purchased in California. Having finished one postcard, Bess reached for another. Out of the corner of her eye, she spotted one postcard slip off the seat and drop to the floor. When she reached down to pick it up, Bess was surprised to find a small pair of eyes looking up at her. Bess squinted into the shadows where she found a small black cat poking its head out from under her seat. The cat slowly stepped out; its head arced up and its bright yellow eyes studied Bess.

"Well, hello there," Bess grinned.

Then, much to Bess's surprise, the cat took one step and jumped up on her granddaughter's lap. Nicole squealed in a surprised tone of excitement and glee. Bess smiled at Nicole's eyes, which grew wider at the sight of the cat. After a couple of seconds, the reality of the situation occurred to Nicole and she started to giggle at the visitor on her lap. The cat turned once and sat down on Nicole's legs in what Bess took to be a gesture of trust and contentment.

"Look at the cat, Mommy!" Nicole spoke with a cautious sense of excitement.

Samantha, who'd been checking her phone, looked over and the expression on her face told Bess she was none too happy about the guest that had joined them.

"Don't touch it," Samantha warned and she shook a finger in Nicole's direction.

"But his fur looks soft," Nicole grinned and she reached up and ran her hand down the back of the cat. "All cats are soft."

"It's dirty," Samantha countered and she shook her head. "It hopped up from the floor, Nicole. It might have been down there for hours. Please don't touch that dirty thing."

"But he likes me," Nicole replied and she looked at the cat and grinned. "See the way he sits on my lap, Mommy. I think he really likes me."

Samantha glanced at Bess, rolled her eyes, and stepped into the aisle. She began to look from one end of the train car to the other, as if searching for more stray cats.

"What are you doing, dear?" Bess asked.

"Checking for the conductor," Samantha replied.

"Why?" Bess asked, placing another postcard on the empty seat beside her.

"To find someone to take this cat away, of course!" Samantha snapped.

Bess glanced around the passenger car. A few people were reading newspapers but no one in uniform appeared to be present. Bess looked at the expression on her daughter's face and shook her head.

"Samantha, dear, please sit down," Bess said.

"Why?" Samantha answered, barely looking at Bess. "I want to get rid of this cat. You know I'm allergic to cats, Mother. They've made me sneeze since I was a girl."

"I know," Bess smiled, "but I believe the cat will be gone soon enough."

"It will when I find the conductor," Samantha stated while she continued to look at both ends of the car for some assistance.

"You don't need the conductor," Bess sighed.

"Do you know what's going to happen when this train stops?" Samantha began, her eyes turning to Nicole. "She's going to want to keep that cat and I'm going to say 'no' and we're going to have a fight about it. I can feel my eyes starting to itch. I need someone to take that cat away now. Isn't there some way of calling for assistance?"

"Samantha...please," Bess said in a soft, calming tone.

When Samantha finally looked down at her, Bess reached up and gently squeezed Samantha's hand.

"Please sit down," Bess quietly suggested.

Samantha stared at her mother, took a deep breath, and then finally agreed to her mother's wish.

"Okay...I'm sitting. Now what do you want me to do, Mother?" Samantha asked.

"Let me explain something to you, my dear," Bess began. "There are no animals allowed in the passenger cars. I was talking to someone in coach yesterday who said their dog is in a carrier in a separate car. Whoever owns this cat is someone who has clearly broken a rule. I'm guessing they'd like to find it before they get in trouble."

Bess and Samantha both turned their eyes to Nicole, who was stroking the cat while grinning and whispering to the animal.

"I like him," Nicole announced to no one in particular. "I'm going to call him Mister Buttons because he has white spots on his black fur that look like buttons. Do you like that name, Mister Buttons?"

The cat turned its head towards Bess and blinked.

"A fine name," Bess said, and she leaned forward in her seat and gently rubbed the cat's head. The cat purred and closed its eyes while Bess rubbed it. "You know, Nicole, this cat belongs to someone else. Someone who misses it terribly. I'm sure they've already named the cat. They might even be looking for it as we speak. When they find us, they might want their cat back."

Nicole put her arms under the cat's chest and carefully lifted it closer to her face.

"I like Mister Buttons. I think he likes me, too," Nicole stated, remaining oblivious to the words Bess had just shared with her.

"Maybe we should give it to the steward in the dining car," Samantha suggested, noting the time on her phone. "We're going there for lunch in a little while. I'm sure someone in the dining car would take it for us."

"I don't think we'll need to wait that long," Bess smiled.

"Why?" Samantha asked.

"Because I suspect Mister Buttons, or whoever he is, has an owner who is very much aware of what has happened," Bess began. "In fact, they're probably worried that someone will find the cat and turn it in. I believe sooner than later we'll see a frantic owner appear in this train car looking high and low for Mister Buttons."

"You seem quite sure of yourself, Mom," Samantha said and she glanced up and down the train car again. "Maybe the owner just doesn't care."

"Oh, I think they do care," Bess replied. "It takes an emotional attachment between a pet and its owner for the owner to smuggle it on a train. That's why I asked you to sit down. You see, my dear, you don't have to go chasing after a rabbit when you're holding the carrot. I think the owner will be here shortly."

"You keep saying that, Mother, but no one is coming," Samantha observed, glancing around the train car again. "Maybe it belongs to someone who's riding in another car."

"I doubt that the owner is sitting back in coach," Bess observed.

"What makes you say that?" Samantha asked. "There are more people riding in coach than in Business Class."

"That's true," Bess nodded. "However, I've walked back there a few times on this trip just to look around. I can tell you that the seats in coach are far too close together. There really is no privacy for someone to break a rule by trying to conceal an animal. No, I have a strong feeling this cat belongs to someone with more room for privacy on this train. I suspect we're looking for someone in business class."

"Mister Buttons is listening to you, Grandma," Nicole warned.

"He must be one of those nosy cats," Bess giggled.

No sooner did Bess look away from Nicole than she spotted a passenger enter their train car. The second the passenger stepped into the car, Bess could tell this was a woman who was in a hurry. Her eyes flicked to the left and then to the right with a nervous rhythm. While Bess had seen some people linger in the doorway to take in their surroundings or to locate a seat, this woman had none of it. She quickly stepped into the train car, her eyes darting around at her surroundings. The question Bess had was whether this woman was looking for a familiar face…or something else?

Bess watched the frantic passenger meander around the car, not taking a seat or talking to anyone. Then her eyes locked on Bess's eyes and she quickly moved in her direction. When she got closer, Bess realized that the woman's eyes were now locked on Nicole, or more specifically, Mister Buttons. The woman paused by their seats, adjusted her glasses and then smiled so broadly it made the wrinkles on her face push up into two sharp points.

"Sebastian, I've been looking everywhere for you," the woman said. She stepped next to Bess and settled into an empty seat beside her and across from Samantha. "Oh, thank heavens. Thank you for finding my cat."

"This is Mister Buttons," Nicole informed the stranger.

"Actually, his name is Sebastian," the woman replied and she pointed towards the neck of the cat. "Did you check his collar, young lady? You'll see Sebastian's name printed right there for everyone to see."

Bess leaned over and noticed the stitching on the cat's blue collar. The stitched lettering did indeed reveal the cat's true name. Bess pointed out the letters to her granddaughter.

"I like Mister Buttons better," Nicole stated.

"I'm sure you do," the woman laughed. "He is a very nice cat."

"You know you're not allowed to bring pets on board the train," Samantha pointed out in a sharp tone of voice. "If the conductor were here I'd report you. I'm allergic to cats. That's why they have that rule...because of people like me. I paid good money for a comfortable trip, not to sneeze all the way home."

"I do apologize," the woman replied, and her eyes flicked around to see if any other passengers reacted to Samantha's loud complaint. "Sebastian just snuck away from me."

"While my granddaughter loves your cat," Bess began, "I'm quite certain she doesn't know the rule that you've broken. There are a good many people who would love to have their pets riding along with them. Why do you feel you're exempt from this rule?"

"I do a lot of travelling in my line of work," the woman explained. "I'm not married. I have no children. Sebastian is my only family. That's why he travels with me. I keep him in a special carry-on bag and in my sleeping quarters. Unfortunately, he slipped out of my cabin when I wasn't looking."

The woman reached over and gently scooped up the cat from Nicole's lap. She smiled at the cat, kissed the top of its head, and then began to unzip a black sweater she was wearing over a navy blue blouse. Bess watched the woman, who was careful to look around before holding Mister Buttons against her blouse and zipping her sweater shut to conceal Mister Buttons. When she was zipped up, the woman crossed her arms at her stomach and stood up.

"Snug as a bug," the woman said to the small bump under her sweater.

Bess thought she looked pregnant in the way her arms looked folded under the round bump of her stomach. Without saying another word, the woman walked away.

"Thank heavens," Samantha mumbled between sniffs and wiping her eyes.

"Goodbye, Mister Buttons!" Nicole called out.

Eventually, Nicole returned to looking out the window, Samantha began to poke at her phone again, and Bess simply returned to filling out her postcards. Then, quite surprisingly, she could feel a smile work its way across her face.

This was the first mystery she'd encountered on her train ride cross-country. Being a former police officer, she always had a keen eye for people. While this particular mystery all but jumped in her lap, she began to look around at the other passengers and her mind began to see them in a different way. Instead of being conscious of their presence as mere background scenery, she began to grow more curious about the details that made up each person. Curiosity always led her to an interesting mystery. It was a long train ride from California to Pennsylvania, Bess told herself.

There were many miles to go and many passengers to watch. Was there another mystery waiting to be found?

Chapter 2: THE DINING CAR

Early on in their travels, Bess discovered one luxury that came with first class train travel was having access to an elegant dining car for three meals a day. From the moment they woke in their sleeping compartment to the time they watched the sunset through a window, Bess, Samantha and Nicole found themselves enjoying the food and the ambience of the dining car.

When they settled into their usual table for lunch, Bess still marveled at the elegant touches that surrounded them—from the crisp white tablecloths to the fine china to the waiters dressed in bright white dress shirts, navy blues ties and matching pants. Once they were seated, Bess, Samantha and Nicole enjoyed the view out the window and the smells that filled the car. They began to talk and the conversation predictably turned to the fate of Mister Buttons.

"Do you think we'll see him again?" Nicole asked.

"I hope not," Samantha mumbled.

"I doubt we will," Bess replied. She turned her eyes to Nicole and smiled. "He was a very nice cat, Nicole, but if Mister Button's owner doesn't want to get into trouble, she will keep her cat safely tucked away in her cabin or a bag or whatever she used to slip him onto the train. If Mister Buttons escapes again, I'm afraid they might take him from his owner."

Nicole's eyes scanned the table, blinked once to process what she'd just heard, and then looked back at Bess.

"I think he likes me," Nicole grinned and her head tipped slightly to one side. "I would take good care of him if he went home with me."

"I'm quite certain you would, my sweet," Bess smiled.

"I'll buy you a fish when we get home," Samantha sighed.

"He liked sitting on me," Nicole recalled. "That's how I know he liked me."

"You smell good, Nicole," Samantha said, kissing Nicole on the head. "That's why he sat on your lap. Animals tend to go to things that smell good."

Nicole grew silent, her large round eyes staring at her mother.

"I still think Mister Buttons likes me," Nicole softly mumbled to herself.

With the Mister Buttons matter resolved, all three ladies turned their eyes outside, where a bright yellow wheat field was perfectly framed by their window.

"I'm hungry," Nicole sighed.

"Yes," Bess nodded. "I am too. When will a waiter come to take our order?"

"Do you know what you're going to have for lunch, Mom?" Samantha asked while she tapped her fingers on the stack of menus on the table. "I've been enjoying the Chicken Caesar salad on this trip. It really is quite good."

"Well," Bess began and she reached over and took one of the menus from the stack, "I've had a hamburger for the last few lunches. Maybe something different would be good."

No sooner had she finished her thought than a waiter arrived to take their order. With no time to waste, Bess quickly ordered a Chicken Caesar salad like Samantha, while Nicole asked for one peanut butter and jelly sandwich.

As they waited for their food, Nicole spoke a little more about Mister Buttons, Samantha revisited the topic of her allergies, and Bess spoke of her recollections of Samantha's allergies when she was younger.

While they talked, Bess could feel the train bank to one side and the sunlight suddenly vanished behind a mountain ridge. She looked out the window to see some mountain goats running along the side of the ridge. The mountain was rounded on top, comprised mostly of rock and dirt, and was bigger than anything Bess had ever seen. When they passed by the mountain, the sun emerged from behind the ridge and daylight poured back into the dining car.

"Look, Mom!" Samantha cried, pointing out the window towards a distant hill filled with lush green color. "Does that look like a vineyard to you?"

"A vineyard?" Bess asked, a little surprised by the question. She squinted into the sunlight striking her window. "I can't tell."

"I think it does," Samantha said. "I think that's a vineyard."

"What's a vineyard?' Nicole asked.

"It's a place where they grow grapes," Samantha explained.

"I like grapes," Nicole grinned and she wiped her nose with the back of her hand.

Nicole quickly turned the conversation from grapes back to Mister Buttons, which Bess was tired of hearing about. She smiled politely but turned her focus to the interior of the train car and away from any more thoughts about the cat. She glanced around to see what the food looked like on the other passengers' plates. Much to her relief, she spotted a passenger looking very happy while she ate a Chicken Caesar salad. The salad looked quite inviting and led Bess to conclude she'd made the right choice for lunch.

Her mind eased in and out of the conversation between Nicole and Samantha while she looked around the dining car. She spotted a few more plates full of inviting food. Then her eyes stopped at one table where she saw a man seated by himself.

He appeared to be middle aged, professionally-dressed in a suit and tie. He slipped off a pair of glasses and tucked them in the vest pocket of his jacket. Bess took a good look at his face and for the briefest of moments she thought she recognized him. Her eyes lingered on his eyes, the shape of his nose, the curve of his jaw, and something inside of her began to grow restless. She turned her eyes back to her table and she could feel her restlessness ease when she heard Nicole talk about her longing for a pet.

A few minutes later, their food arrived. Her first bite of the salad told Bess she'd made a good choice. While she ate, she joined in with her daughter and granddaughter in a conversation about possible pets, the scenery, and the reviews of what each of them had ordered.

Across from where they sat, Bess quickly glanced over to the man she'd been watching. Still seated at the table by himself, he appeared to be finishing his meal. When he was done, she watched him stand up, thank the waiter for a delicious meal and move towards the exit. As he moved through the dining car, Bess quickly put her fork down, wiped her lips, and let her eyes settle on him as he walked by their table.

With conversations from other tables filling the air, Bess found her mind completely engaged by what she'd just seen. To other people, he may have appeared to be a man simply finishing his dinner and leaving. To Bess, it was more than that. She had now realized that this man had done something very clever during his time on the train. Her mind raced and she longed to confront him about his cleverness. While she appeared to be the picture of contentment for her daughter and granddaughter, Bess felt a much greater sense of determination to find this man again.

Chapter 3: CURIOSITY ON A TRAIN

Most people on a train look outside. They look out at the vistas that are perfectly framed by their window. They marvel at how the land seems to unfold itself from one horizon before neatly tucking itself away in the other. Most anyone on a train finds their eyes drawn to the mountains, the valleys, the open fields, and the broad blue sky that eventually frays into ribbons of pink, gold and violet by day's end. While the views from a train can stir the emotions of most any passenger, there was one passenger who no longer cared to indulge in such things.

After two days on an eastbound train, Bess found her eyes lingering more on the faces of the other passengers. As a casual observer, she saw a wide range of people. There were people traveling for work and people traveling for leisure. People for whom train travel was a necessity and people for whom it was more of a leisure activity.

For the days that she spent riding back to Pennsylvania, she'd managed to find a few passengers who were more engaging to study than any scenery flowing by her window. This was not a slight to the natural beauty of the land. More than anything else, it was a tribute to how drawn Bess was to the behavior of others.

At the moment, her eyes were settled on her daughter, Samantha, and her granddaughter, Nicole. Samantha was reading a book. Nicole was staring out the window. Bess leaned her head against the back of the seat while she smiled at her two girls. With time to herself, she began to reflect on the events that had led her to board this train.

It had begun weeks earlier when Bess had received news that her younger brother, Donald, had passed away. It's always a shock when an older sibling learns that a younger sibling has died. Bess knew that Donald had been a heavy smoker for most of his life. From that standpoint, she could rationalize the circumstances surrounding his death. Yet, on a deeply personal level, her heart ached when she learned of her little brother's demise. It simply went against the laws of nature, Bess thought. Older siblings should always die first.

When the idea came up to travel from Pennsylvania to California for the funeral, Bess was hesitant to embrace the challenge. At eighty-one years of age, she knew it would be a difficult journey. Perhaps it was old age, Bess thought, but climbing on a jet did not sound all that appealing to her. She enjoyed a good car ride, but driving to California was simply too difficult a trip to make. When Bess's daughter suggested a three-day train ride to California, Bess considered it the best option. As soon as she committed herself to the idea of riding on a train, she became excited about the prospects of doing a long trip with her daughter and granddaughter.

The trip out west went smoother than Bess had expected. For the three day journey to California, she'd enjoyed her sleeping cabin, the foods they served in the dining car, and the time to spend chatting with her daughter and granddaughter. She also occupied her mind with memories of Donald.

Bess could easily recall the days when she and Donald had run around their neighborhood as children. She had vivid memories of the adventures they'd gone on, the friends they'd made and the secrets they'd kept.

She could still see herself as a child helping little Donald sell lemonade, fruit, or fresh tomatoes in their neighborhood to earn money. Even as a child, Donald always had a good head for business.

When they were at the funeral, Bess found herself relaying these stories over and over again to Donald's children and his widow. They were stories from the heart. Nuggets of childhood memories that she'd bring up to anyone who would listen. They were memories that conveyed his spirit as a child with his gift for business. More than once at the funeral, Bess remarked how Donald could always find a way to make money. Having led a successful life in business, it was clear to Bess that Donald's instincts had simply grown sharper with age.

Memories of the funeral service filled her mind on the train ride home. The words that were spoken and the memories that were shared touched her and lingered with her for most of the ride home. After experiencing so much sadness and grief, Bess felt drained. She drew in her breath and let her eyes rest on her granddaughter, Nicole, who was curled up on her seat with her eyes glued to the window.

"How are you doing, Mom?" Samantha asked, looking up from a book she was reading. She put the book on her lap, reached across and put her hand on Bess's hand. "You look tired. It's been a long trip. A few days on a train, not to mention Uncle Donald's funeral…you must be exhausted."

"I'm fine," Bess smiled. "It'll be good to get back and see Chet. I hope his back is feeling better. You know he hasn't been able to go to Waltzing Club in weeks because of a nerve in his back. The doctors told him to rest and that's what he's doing. Poor dear. He really wanted to come along."

"I know not having him along has made this trip a little harder on you," Samantha observed, sitting back in her seat. "When we first talked about doing it, you didn't seem all that interested in going. What changed your mind?"

"Well, of course, it was my brother," Bess explained. "That was a factor. I wanted to be there to honor his memory, but then I'd think about the trip. Even by train, I knew it was quite long and I wasn't certain about doing it. I honestly didn't know what to do. Then one day you brought Nicole around to visit me. At one point, she noticed that I was taking my afternoon nap on the couch while she was watching TV. When I opened my eyes, I saw her standing right in front of me. Do you remember that day, Nicole?"

Nicole merely grinned at Bess, but didn't offer a word.

"So there she was, staring right at me, and she asked me a question," Bess recalled. "Do you remember what you asked?"

Nicole thought for a few seconds before shaking her head from side to side.

"You asked me if I was sleeping," Bess recalled. "I told her I was, and then she asked me if I ever dreamed when I slept. I told her I did. When she asked what I dreamed about I told her I dreamed about the same things that other people dreamed of; the places I'd like to visit and the people I'd like to meet. Well, Nicole's eyes blinked twice, as if I'd said something wrong. Then she quickly informed me that I didn't really go anywhere and that I didn't ever meet new people because all I did was stay in my house. On some level...it occurred to me she was right. That's when I knew I had to push myself to make this trip. I had to do it for Donald...and to get out of my comfort zone one more time."

When she finished speaking, Bess looked at Nicole. She reached out and gently brushed the top of her granddaughter's head. Her auburn hair was soft to the touch. Bess could tell Nicole's eyes were fixed on a large snow-capped mountain in the distance.

"Such a wise little thing," Bess sighed.

Her eyes lingered on Nicole. Bess couldn't help but marvel at how a simple word or smile from her granddaughter could touch her heart in such a direct way. As she grinned at her granddaughter, Bess spotted a figure moving down the main aisle of the train car. At first, it was simply a dot in the corner of her eye. As the figure drew larger, Bess turned her eyes and got a better view of the approaching passenger. After a few seconds, the person came into view and Bess quickly recognized him as the man from the dining car.

To most passengers, Bess thought, he appeared to be a typical businessman strolling through the car. Dressed in a nice suit with slicked back dark hair and an urgent stride, he fit right in with the other business passengers on the train. Yet, his face still looked familiar to Bess. While she was never good with names, her mind was quite good at taking snapshots of anyone she met. She knew she'd met him before.

"That man," Bess said and she gestured towards the aisle where he was walking. "Do you remember him, Samantha?"

"No," Samantha said, glancing at the aisle for a few seconds before turning her attention back to her phone. "I don't remember ever seeing him."

"I believe we did," Bess mumbled to herself. "I believe all three of us have met him."

"I haven't," Samantha mumbled before poking at her phone.

Bess sat back and smiled at her daughter. Once again, technology had distracted her away from a small detail that Bess found to be quite interesting. She glanced back out to the aisle, watched him walk away, and then turned her eyes back to Samantha.

"Would you excuse me?" Bess said and she stood up after speaking.

"Where are you going, Mother?' Samantha asked, still staring at her phone.

"I'm going to the bathroom," Bess answered and she offered Samantha a comforting smile, which Samantha looked at for a split second before turning back to her phone.

Samantha shifted her legs to the side and Bess managed to step out into the aisle.

Ahead of her, Bess saw the object of her interest. She took a deep breath, looked at the stranger up ahead and decided to indulge her curious nature.

The rhythmic sound of metal wheels tapping on train tracks was something Bess had grown accustomed to hearing during her trip. The tapping sound filled the air with the same recurring pattern both day and night. It had become as natural to her as the scenery out the window or the faces of the other passengers.

Passing through the train car, she barely drew a glance from the other passengers. Bess could easily recall a time when she could catch the eye of any young man when she walked by. However, old age caused her blond hair to turn gray, her shapely legs to fill with blue veins, and her fashion tastes to become more sensible. While time had taken away her natural good looks, it had replaced her beauty with a less obvious gift: anonymity. It was a gift that Bess had grown fond of. It complemented her nature to observe people and investigate their curious behaviors.

She watched the man in front of her maintain an easy pace, taking slow relaxed strides through one train car before moving into another one. Bess struggled to keep up. Occasionally, the train car would bounce or shift, causing her to grab hold of the nearest thing to maintain her balance. After one too many bounces, her arthritic knee began to flare. She paused in an aisle. She watched the man step ahead of her. The pain in her knee subsided and she resumed her pursuit.

Passing through two, three, four train cars, Bess kept up with the focus of her interest. She watched his every step and took particular interest in the unique way he walked. She also began to notice how each car was laid out differently.

She followed him through one train car that had seats arranged to face each other, encouraging passengers to socialize. She kept up with him though another train car where she found seats facing towards the front of the train in straight rows. Perhaps, Bess thought, this was for those people who wanted to minimize their social experience. She glanced down one row where she saw a few people staring at their phones and enjoying their privacy.

Bess followed him into yet another car. This time she discovered seats that were facing long broad windows that extended from the floor to the ceiling. This train car was clearly dedicated to those passengers who wanted to enjoy the views, Bess thought. She watched the man she was pursuing settle into a chair facing one of the windows that framed a vast open desert. She drew in her breath and walked up to her subject. She stopped next to an empty chair where the stranger was seated.

Bess glanced out the windows and took a moment to let her mind produce the right words to say. She studied him, noting his perfectly shined black shoes, his navy blue suit and how it accented his bright orange tie. He was clean-shaven. His dark hair was slicked back with hair gel, giving him a sleek professional appearance.

All of it, taken as a whole, was not that unusual. However, it was the subtle clues that made this man interesting to her. It was the mystery of his nuanced transformation that drew her to him. She took a deep breath and stepped up to where the man was seated and she folded her hands in front of her waist.

"It certainly looks lovely out there," Bess sighed and she gestured to the windows.

"Yes, it does," the man replied, pulling out his phone and checking the screen.

"Are you from California?" Bess asked, settling into a chair next to the stranger.

"I was there for work," the man replied, frowning at something on his cell phone's screen before tucking it away in his jacket pocket. "California is nice to visit, but Pennsylvania is where I call home."

"What a coincidence," Bess smiled. "Pennsylvania is my home, too. I took a trip out to California with my daughter and granddaughter, but I live in a retirement home in the Pennsylvania Dutch Country."

"Well, then, this is quite a trip for you and your family," the man nodded and he mustered a slight smile. "A memorable vacation to see the country."

"I wish it was a vacation," Bess stated. "I'm afraid, like you, I had another reason for making this trip. You see, I went to California because my brother died."

"Oh, I'm sorry," the man said and he pressed his lips together after finishing his comment. His eyes turned out the window and a pause began to settle between them.

"You know," Bess said, leaning forward in her seat. "I believe we've met before."

"I'm afraid you're mistaken," the man mumbled and he checked his watch before folding his hands on his lap and letting a big yawn escape. "I'm going to grab some sleep, if you don't mind. It was nice meeting you.

You can stay if you want, ma'am, but please don't talk to me anymore. We're going to be in Pennsylvania in a couple hours and I need some rest. I have a lot of meetings to attend when I get back to the office."

With those words, the man did exactly as promised. He tilted his head back slightly, folded his arms across his chest and closed his eyes. Bess watched him for a few seconds. She turned and glanced around at the other passengers, but her mind was racing. After a minute, she simply couldn't help herself.

"I'm sorry," Bess blurted out, turning back to the man. "I know you asked me to be quiet but I just can't help thinking that we've met before."

The man's eyes opened slightly.

"Please," the man sighed. "I need some sleep."

"I'm sorry," Bess replied. "But when I get something stuck in my head, it just stays there until I can do something about it."

"I see," the man sighed and he shook his head at the situation he found himself in. "I'd get up and leave but you've already followed me through five cars. In fact, I'll bet you'll probably get right up and follow me if I started walking again."

Bess smiled.

"Okay," he mumbled and he rubbed his eyes. He sat up a little in his seat then looked her up and down once. "You seem to be too old to be a stalker. So you're bothering me because…you think we've met?"

"That's one reason…but I do have another excuse for shamelessly chasing after you," Bess said and she smiled again to cut through the tension that she sensed building between them.

"And what might that be?" the man asked.

"You see, in the days since we've left California," Bess began. "I've noticed how you've changed."

The observation hung in the air without any response from her subject. Bess could see how he was staring at her, waiting for her to continue. She drew in her breath, arranged her thoughts, and then continued.

"Over the last few days, I spotted you in different places on the train," Bess began. "I've passed you in the aisle, caught a glimpse of you in the dining car, even found you seated a few times when I was passing through a car with my granddaughter. Every time I'd see you, something about you would change."

"Oh, really?" the man finally mumbled. "I'm still the same man I was a few days ago. The way you're talking, you'd think I was turning into a woman or something."

"Nothing that drastic," Bess laughed. "It was a more subtle transformation. One day, I noticed that you changed your clothes from something casual to something more formal.

Another day, I saw that your hair went from being curly and wavy to more stylized. On another day, we passed each other in the aisle and I saw that a wedding band had appeared on your finger. Even your glasses have been replaced with contact lenses. On their own, these are all subtle changes that most people would miss. Taken as a whole, I find it to be quite a fascinating change in appearance."

"I don't recall ever meeting you," the man said and he leaned his head back and closed his eyes. "Now, would you please go away?"

"You may be right," Bess nodded. "We've never formally met or been introduced. Yet, I'm confident in saying that we have a mutual acquaintance."

"What makes you say that?" the man quickly asked, opening his eyes.

"It started a few days ago when I first entered the train in California," Bess explained and she looked him in the eye. "I had just boarded the train and was walking to my seat with my daughter and granddaughter. Now, of course, my granddaughter, Nicole, is very young and like all young children her feet tends to be two seconds ahead of her brain. That's why when she was rushing ahead of us to find our seats she tripped and fell in the aisle. It was a terrible fall. She practically landed on her face. Before her mother and I could help her, this nice man, a total stranger, pulled my granddaughter to her feet and asked her if she was okay. That nice man had wavy dark hair, glasses, and was wearing shorts and a flowery shirt like he'd been to Hawaii. That man...was you. You glanced at my face for a second, then left before I could thank you."

"I'm afraid you're mistaken," the man answered with a voice that was softer and he turned his eyes out the nearest window.

"When you walk, do you know you have a slight limp to the right?" Bess asked.

The man looked down at his phone and stroked the screen with his thumb.

"That's why I followed you," Bess continued. "I wasn't stalking you...I was studying how you walked to be certain of that same distinct gait. You really do bear more weight on your right leg. Did you injure your leg at some point in your life?"

The man said nothing in reply to her observation.

"My granddaughter is very precious to me," Bess continued. "When you took the time to stop, reach down and help her, it caught my attention. Unfortunately, I never had a chance to thank you. I kept looking for you on the train to express my gratitude, but every time I saw you, the changes I noticed were distracting me. Despite your suit, your contact lenses, and your hair, I was still able to notice that same distinct walk this morning."

Still the man said nothing to her comments.

"When I spotted you leaving the dining car the other day, I saw one more thing that forced me into confronting you," Bess continued. "I saw a wedding band that was on your finger. It's the first time I'd seen the ring since we left California. It left me to wonder…why?"

"Why what?"

"Why would such a kind man cheat on his wife?" Bess replied.

She couldn't help but notice that her words were met with silence. She watched the man slowly put down his phone and turn his eyes out the window. The tapping sound of the train's wheels suddenly seemed to grow in volume to Bess. She thought he looked like someone who'd been trapped by logic and reason. She also knew she wasn't going to give him an inch. She wanted the truth. Waiting for a response, Bess wondered what words he would use in reply to her comments. What excuses would he offer for his curious behavior?

His eyes turned towards her. His mouth began to part. The expression on his face told her she was about to learn the truth. Whatever words were about to leave his lips, Bess knew they would be words that would make for an interesting story to share with her friends at the Honey Hills Retirement Center.

Chapter 4: THE REST OF THE STORY

Home. The word has a different meaning for each person. For Bess, "home" had always been a warm and friendly place where she felt like she belonged. Fortunately for her, there were two such places that fit this description.

The first "home" was a small ranch house located on the grounds of the Honey Hills Retirement Center. Tucked along Dogwood Lane was the home that Bess shared with her loving husband, Chet. While she enjoyed the cozy confines of her home, she felt blessed to have another place that was also warm and welcoming.

Her second "home" was a bit more intimate. Once a week, Bess met with a small group of fellow residents to play bridge. They called their group "The Honey Hills Bridge Club," and they tried to meet at least once a week. While it wasn't a traditional home, it was still a place that was warm and friendly and made Bess feel welcome. For someone grieving the loss of a brother, both places were good medicine for a heart in mourning.

She returned from her train trip on a Monday night. When she woke on a Tuesday morning, Bess was quick to call her friends to tell them she was home and ready to play cards. She was quite excited to see Rose Grumbine, Flo Morgenstern, and Alma Crisp. She was also excited to tell them about her westward excursion.

Walking from her home to the main building, Bess grinned at the thought of her impending meeting. She paid little attention to the bright blue sky, the colorful trees, and the mild autumn air. At this time of the year, she no longer had to rise early to beat the blistering summer sun for a morning walk. The air was dry and the morning sun golden.

"Perfect," Bess mumbled to herself about the conditions.

On the way to her Bridge Club meeting, she walked by a tree with full green leaves, one of the few trees that hadn't started to change colors with the season. She noticed a red spot on one branch. At first, she thought it was a red leaf, but soon realized it was a cardinal perched on a tree branch. The sounds of the bird's song made Bess smile and her footsteps slowed just a bit so she could enjoy the melody. After a few seconds, she resumed her pace to the main building for her meeting.

Once inside the main building, she picked up her pace. She smiled and said "hello" to a few acquaintances who she recognized in the halls. When she arrived in the game room, her friends were waiting. Smiles and hugs were quickly exchanged. Greetings were shared. Warm words flowed and soon they all sat down for a game of bridge.

While the first hand was dealt, Bess found the conversation moved with the kind of natural flow that tended to happen between friends. At first, it was with easy, broad queries about her trip. How was the train ride? How was the food? How well did she sleep at night?

After some polite conversation over Bess's answers, she could sense that the questions were becoming more thoughtful and more intimate. Soon she entertained questions about the funeral, questions about her feelings on burying her brother, and questions about her grief. Living in a retirement home, death was usually not a topic of conversation that Bess indulged in with other residents. Today was different.

"Were you close to your brother?" Rose asked. "With him living in California, I can't imagine you saw him that much."

"The last time I saw him was the day I married Chet," Bess smiled. "It was a good day. When he went back home, we made a promise to call each other once a week. We kept that promise. It was good to hear his voice every week. Part of me thinks if I went back to my room and called his number, he'd still be there to pick up the phone."

No one knew what to say after Bess spoke those words. She could sense the unintended tension in the air her words had created.

"He was a good brother." Bess nodded to her cards, choosing not to make eye contact with her friends. "I'll always have good memories of Donald to keep with me."

"Well, we're happy you're back," Rose sighed.

"Yes," Alma chimed in. "Glad you're here. I, for one, missed playing cards with you."

"Thank you." Bess nodded. "Were you able to have any meetings while I was gone? I know you needed a fourth for bridge. I was just curious…did you have any luck finding someone to replace me?"

"We tried," Rose said.

"Oh, how we tried," Flo mumbled while rubbing her forehead.

"Really?" Bess asked, feeling her curiosity grow. "So, how did that go?"

"Not well!" Flo blurted out.

"Now, Flo, it wasn't *that* bad," Rose said, and she shot a disapproving look at Flo from across the table.

"Well," Rose began, "first we called Delores Jackson. She lives just down the hallway from me.

Delores is a skilled conversationalist and I thought she would be a wonderful addition. Unfortunately, I didn't realize how poor her vision was."

"She kept asking us to help her read the cards in her hand," Flo complained. "Now what kind of game was that? Everyone took turns getting up to help her read her cards. That was a waste of a morning."

"It was a bit bothersome." Rose nodded. "So the following week we decided to ask Althea Clarkson to play with us. Althea is always quite friendly in the Dining Hall and her eyesight is quite good when she orders from the menu. Unfortunately, I didn't realize she was having….other problems."

"What kind of problems?" Bess asked.

"She kept talking about putting her cat in a mason jar," Alma said and she shook her head after the comment. "Then she told us how when she dies she wants to be put in a mason jar before she gets buried. She really likes mason jars."

"Well." Flo smiled. "Where to begin with that commentary? I explained to Althea that a cat cannot fit in a mason jar. I also tried to explain to her that she wouldn't fit into a mason jar. Well, that just got her all upset with me. We argued after the first round of cards and then she just got up from the table and walked out on us."

"Yes." Rose nodded. "That was our briefest game of bridge this year."

"I'm afraid Althea won't be joining us again," Alma stated. "I believe I heard she's in the Dementia Unit now."

"With a mason jar I'm sure," Flo giggled.

"I'm so sorry to hear that," Bess said, shaking her head at all the news. "It's a shame you had so many problems. I'm glad I came back, though. It sounds like you were running out of people to replace me with."

"We were." Alma nodded. "It was a real mystery trying to find someone to replace you. Speaking of mysteries...did you have any...curious moments on your trip? I mean, nothing like passengers talking about stuffing themselves in mason jars, but....anything unusual that you'd like to share with us?"

"Unusual in what way?" Bess asked.

"Oh, don't be dim, Bess. You know what she means," Flo grumbled.

"I'm afraid I don't," Bess answered.

"Alma hasn't been able to write in her blog since you left," Rose reported. "Without you around to solve mysteries, Alma hasn't been able to post anything new on her website."

"Now, ladies," Alma snapped, a hint of annoyance creeping into her voice, "It's not like that at all. I'm not fishing for stories from Bess. I was just making conversation."

Bess smiled at the welcome change in the conversation. Rather than focusing on her grief, the ladies were curious about other aspects of her trip. Talking about a little mystery was just what Bess needed to do. She smiled at Alma, who'd started a blog about the mysteries Bess solved around Honey Hills. Most of the residents read the blog. At first, Bess was not comfortable with the attention Alma's website was putting on her. Over time, Bess's feelings changed about Alma's blog. She began to see it as a compliment and quite enjoyed talking to other residents about her numerous investigations.

Bess slowly turned to her cards and played one card in a very matter of fact way. She then took a deep breath and looked at Alma, whose mouth was hanging open in anticipation of an answer to her question.

"Well, I did find one rock formation out in the deserts of New Mexico to be rather curious," Bess recalled with a grin. "A mountain that looked like a pile of children's building blocks. Just fascinating, Alma. I must say, ladies, after seeing miles and miles of desert and jagged rocky mountains, I'm very happy to be surrounded by the rolling green hills of Pennsylvania again."

"So a pile of rocks?" Alma asked. "That was your big mystery?"

"Oh, I did have one curious encounter with a passenger," Bess began. She smiled a little and looked at Alma. "One little mystery that I resolved. You see…there was this man."

"Was he cute?' Rose asked.

"Cute and single?" Alma joined in.

"She's married, ladies!" Flo snapped.

"That's true, Flo," Bess answered. "Yet, there's something romantic about spying on a stranger when riding a train. Especially a subtle stranger."

"What do you mean by *subtle*?" Flo asked.

"Subtle in his appearance," Bess replied.

"I don't understand," Flo mumbled.

"You see, what interested me about him was how many small things changed in his appearance on the trip back to Pennsylvania," Bess explained.

"What things changed?" Rose leaned in.

"Oh my…where to start?" Bess began and she lowered the cards she was holding. "I'd suppose the first thing to change were his clothes. When we left California he was dressed like a casual beachgoer. You know the kind…flowery shirt, shorts, flip-flops. As we got closer to Pennsylvania, he began to change."

"How?" Alma asked.

"He started to wear business suits and well-polished shoes," Bess recalled. "Then there were his glasses, which he wore when we left California but chose to replace with contact lenses when we got closer to the end of our trip. One day I noticed his hair even changed."

"Did he cut it?" Alma asked.

"Nothing that drastic," Bess replied, glancing across the table at Alma. "Instead, he simply used some styling gel to slick his hair back. The final straw came when I noticed a little thing that most of the other passengers wouldn't have picked up on."

"What was that?" Rose joined in.

"I saw that he had placed a wedding ring on his finger," Bess recalled. She looked around the table and nodded. "When that last detail revealed itself to me, that's when I knew."

"Knew what?" Flo finally spoke up.

"I knew that this man had a secret," Bess explained. "I now knew there had to be a reason behind his transformation. Of course, I was curious. I wanted to learn more. I wanted to understand and confirm my suspicions for all of these little changes that I'd observed. So one day, I followed him through some train cars and confronted him. I wanted to learn the truth. Eventually I was able to track him down."

"And what did he do?" Flo asked.

"When I found him, he was seated by a window," Bess recalled. "He was staring out at a stretch of desert that we were traveling through. It really was quite a lovely scene. I even found my eyes lingering on the jagged mountains and the open landscape for a few seconds. Something in my mind clicked and my eyes quickly turned back to the subject of my pursuit."

"What did he do when he saw you?" Rose asked.

"When I approached him," Bess recalled, "I could tell by the expression on his face that he was annoyed with me. We had just spoken casually a few minutes earlier and now I was going to bother him again. He appeared none too happy about it but I didn't care. I wanted to get to the heart of the matter."

"So was he angry with you?" Rose asked.

"Not angry…maybe 'quietly annoyed' would be a better term," Bess replied. "He mumbled a few choice words to express his annoyance."

"Didn't that bother you?" Alma asked. "I know when someone is annoyed with me it weighs on me until I can make amends."

"I ignored the expression on his face," Bess explained. "I sat down in a chair next to him, considered his annoyance, and then thought about what to say first."

"I'm surprised he didn't stand up to leave," Flo stated.

"I think he was tired of having me follow him," Bess quickly answered. "He was a bit more confrontational with me when I tracked him down the second time. I noticed that by the first words he said to me."

"And what were they?' Alma asked.

"He told me if I was a man he'd have slugged me for following him," Bess recalled.

The other three ladies at the table put their cards down after hearing that comment.

"How rude!" Rose chimed in.

"I agree," Alma said, her hand practically covering her mouth. "I don't care how angry someone is, it doesn't give them the right to say such things to a lady."

"Quite true." Bess nodded. "I don't think it was anger that led him to choose those words. You see, ladies, this was a man who had a secret and I could sense he was trying to guard it. I put on my best smile to try to put him at ease. As an old woman, I do find that my smile and my pleasant demeanor put many people at ease. That's one of the trappings that comes with old age, I guess."

"Did it work?' Rose asked.

Bess drew in her breath, looked around at her friends, and quickly assembled the events in her mind that she was about to convey.

"After I gave him my warmest smile, I told him what I had observed," Bess began. "I explained how, over the course of our train ride from California to Pennsylvania, I had seen his clothes change, his hair change, his glasses disappear and a wedding ring appear on his finger. I was intent on making it quite clear to him that I noticed all of these little details and was curious about them."

"And what did he think about your observations?" Alma asked.

"He called me a nosey old lady," Bess replied

"Well, that wasn't very nice," Rose sighed.

"I didn't mind," Bess sighed and she shrugged her shoulders. "In fact, it was the first clue I had that I was onto something. The second clue came when he stopped looking at his cell phone. It was a gesture that told me I had his complete attention."

"Then what happened?" Rose asked.

"I told him everything. When I'd first noticed him on the day we boarded the train. How he'd caught my eye by an act of kindness I'd seen him commit when Nicole fell and he helped her," Bess stated.

Bess paused and looked around the table.

"You know, my mother was the best person I knew," Bess explained. "She once told me that the measure of a person wasn't by what they said, but by their manners. I told him I'd seen the way he'd helped my granddaughter when she'd boarded the train and fell trying to find our seats. Then I sat back in my seat and took a deep breath after sharing this recollection."

"I told him there was no hesitation in what he did," Bess went on to explain. "I believe he responded to my granddaughter's fall from the heart. It was one thing to help her up, but quite another to brush off the dirt and say something kind to her to help her stop crying. I think acts like that are windows into a person's heart; at least that's what my mother used to say. Judging by those few seconds, I believed him to be a genuinely good person. That's what fascinated me."

"How so?" Rose asked.

"You see, I believed he was cheating on his wife," Bess explained, "which is the obvious deduction to make when a man removes his wedding ring and then puts it back on. His changing appearance only reinforced that belief. What I found interesting about him was how difficult it must have been for a person with such a good heart to live with so much deception."

"Did you say that to him?" Flo asked.

"I did," Bess replied.

"You told him you thought he was cheating on his wife?" Rose asked.

"I did," Bess smiled.

"Oh, Bess," Flo laughed and she shook her head in disbelief. "You're braver than me."

"So what did he say about your accusation?" Alma asked. "Did he threaten to punch you again?"

"His words were very clear and direct," Bess recalled. "He looked right at me and asked me why I would say something so rude. I told him straight away that it was based on what I'd seen him do on our trip back from California."

"And then what happened?" Alma asked.

Bess looked around at her friends, none of whom were looking at their cards or even thinking about playing bridge. They all were hanging on every word of her story. She reflected on her memories and began to share everything she could recall.

Chapter 5: REMEMBERING THE STRANGER ON THE TRAIN

I can still recall how he sighed when he looked at me. It wasn't a sigh of disgust as much as it was relief. I watched his eyes scan the train car, then he looked back at me with an expression that made me feel like I was some kind of fish he'd caught. I wasn't sure if I was about to be released with a few kind words or reamed out with anger. He sat up in his seat and scanned the train car one more time to see how many people were near us. After a minute, his eyes glanced down at his shoes and he sighed.

"I have a complicated life," he told me in a soft voice. "It's complicated *because* of that "good" heart you're talking about."

I sensed his guard was still up so I gestured around to the other passengers who were either looking out windows or talking on cell phones. I pointed them out and told him no one was listening to us. No one else cared. I reminded him I didn't even know his name and that he didn't know mine, which made it the perfect situation for us to talk.

I can still remember how that man shifted in his seat with an uncomfortable expression on his face. He looked like someone who was sitting on a fork or something else unpleasant. Then I remember how this smile slowly crept across his rigid face. His eyes relaxed and I could actually see for the first time that his eyes were brown. The tension on his face appeared to have melted away.

"Why not," he said a little louder and he leaned back in his seat and looked a bit more at ease with me. He rubbed his hands together like they were cool and nodded. "It's been too long since I confessed my sins to God or anyone else. Like you said, we don't know each other. I'd suppose confessing to a stranger wouldn't hurt. You say you live in a retirement home?"

I nodded my head.

"All the better," he grinned.

He looked around to check one more time for anyone close to us, then rested his elbows on his knees.

"I travel a good bit for my job," he began and he tucked his phone into his coat pocket. "I live on the east coast but for the last few years, I've been travelling out west to oversee a new plant my company is building. I don't like to fly so my company arranged for me to take a train. Shortly after going out there, I met someone at a restaurant. Did you ever meet someone…and the conversation just sparked? I mean sparked from the first word to the last? That's what I found in this lovely young lady I met."

Of course, I held the judgment riding on my tongue. Instead, I just smiled and nodded to encourage him to continue.

"Then you know what it's like," the man replied and he smiled just a bit. "I found myself staring at her blue eyes and laughing when she laughed. While we talked, she told me she owned a winery where my company was planning to hold a retreat. For the next few days, we spent more time together going over details of the retreat. The closer we worked together, the more we fell in love."

"What was it about her?" I asked.

"When we first met, I loved that she was sweet and young and passionate about everything. Those were the same qualities that attracted me to my wife many years earlier," he explained.

"Don't you still love those qualities about your wife?" I whispered, mindful of the need for discretion in talking about such matters.

"Those qualities are gone," the man sighed and his face lost all expression. "A long marriage, raising children…those kinds of experiences can change a person. It changed my wife. Those qualities I fell in love with…her easy nature and her laughter…they were replaced by constant worrying and nagging."

When he told me this, the expression on his face and the tone in his voice actually made me feel a bit sorry for him. He looked like someone who had lost something special. Something that he knew he'd never get back again.

"Perhaps a change of scenery would help you and your wife," I suggested. "California is a lovely place. Warm weather year round just might mellow her."

"I asked my wife to move to California," the man explained. "With this project I'm working on, I spent a good bit of time designing and overseeing the construction of this plant. I suggested we move the family to the west coast. She told me to think of the children and the friendships they had at school. She wanted our life to stay the same."

"So you agreed to her demands?" Bess asked.

"I've always been the provider for our family," the man explained and he turned his eyes out a nearby window to collect his thoughts. "You know, when you spend your life doing this, earning money for a family, it's like you maintain this cocoon so that the family's way of life doesn't change. They can still belong to the country club. They can still take riding lessons. They can still have the things that are important to them. Those things just aren't important to me anymore."

"So what about your life in California?" I asked.

"Because she owns her own business, my California girl is passionate about wine and running her vineyard. She isn't interested in frivolous things like social status, designer clothes, and finding out the latest rumor. She's young and she has her whole future in front of her. She loves her business and pours herself into it."

"I see," I answered.

"Now, do I love my wife, my children, and the experience of being part of a family? Of course I do," he said in a softer voice. "I'm not embarrassed to say that it also feels good to share my life with a younger woman. There's something about young love that makes each day feel...exciting, energizing, youthful."

When I heard those words, my brief moment of sympathy was gone. When you reach my age, you realize that youthful love is always more attractive, but never lasting.

"So you find your life in California...satisfying?" I asked.

"My California girl is a breath of fresh air for me," the man explained. "You see, she loves me for the person I am and not just for what I can provide. My wife used to love me that way. Somewhere through the years she began to value the things I could buy more than how much she loved me."

He stopped, laughed a little and shook his head, perhaps reflecting on his words.

"Did I say something funny?" I asked.

"No," the man replied. "It's just that I can't believe I'm sharing all of this with a total stranger. I don't know how I got to the point in my life where I'm telling a little old lady my deepest thoughts. Maybe it's because I don't know you. I gotta tell you, though, it does feel good to unburden on someone. I've been keeping this a secret for a long time. It feels good to let it out."

"I can imagine it must be hard for you," I said in the best sympathetic tone I could muster for any rascal cheating on his wife. "It must be terribly difficult living with half a heart on the west coast and half a heart on the east coast."

"I love both of my lives. I'll keep it that way for as long as I can," the man stated. Out of nowhere, I heard this chirping sound fill the air between us. My eyes looked around before I saw the stranger reach into his jacket pocket and pull out his phone. He checked the message on the screen.

"I've enjoyed our conversation…but I really must ask you to leave now," the man stated, still staring at his phone. "This is a business call, ma'am. It's from a contractor in California who's supplying our company with materials for our new plant. He's late on an order and I'm going to have to use some colorful language to motivate him."

"Of course," I answered, sensing that he had nothing more to offer me.

As I walked away, I thought about how I pass strangers every day. How I pass them on my morning walks. How I see them at the retirement home. I never stop to consider how simple or challenging their lives are. There are always people who make life more complicated for themselves by the choices they make and the secrets they keep. A subtle stranger on a train reminded me of this fact.

Chapter 6: THE OPEN HEART

When Bess finished her story, she glanced around the table. Flo still had her cards up, studying them with the same intensity that she'd been doing before Bess began her story. Alma and Rose were less interested in their cards, their eyes clearly focused on Bess and her story.

"I wouldn't have had the nerve to confront someone like that," Rose stated, and she shook her head to emphasize her point.

"Me neither," Alma agreed and her eyes narrowed behind her glasses. "You walked right up to a stranger you suspected was cheating on his wife and confronted him about it? My goodness, Bess, you've got nerve."

"Not smart," Flo spoke up from behind her cards. "You're a little thing, Bess. You're lucky he didn't hurt you."

"The facts told me I wasn't wrong." Bess shrugged. "I was confident he was cheating and my observations reinforced that belief. What I have found over the years is that when an observation leads me to a suspicion...my suspicions tend to be true."

"You got lucky he didn't get mad and hit you," Flo mumbled.

"I'm old, short and I have a very slender build, Flo," Bess replied. "Punching a little old lady would have only gotten him unwanted attention from the other passengers on the train. I knew that. It would have been attention he didn't want. I was very aware of that when I decided to confront him. Besides, I suspected he had more kindness in his heart than anger. Another suspicion that turned out to be true."

"Oh, Bess, you're braver than me," Alma grinned.

With her story completed, silence crept over the table as the focus of each player was drawn back into a round of cards. Bess looked around the table and smiled. While riding on a train and meeting new people had been a fun experience, it felt good to be surrounded by familiar faces again.

"Well, Alma has some surprising news for you, Bess," Rose finally spoke up. Her eyes turned to Alma after finishing her statement. "Go ahead, Alma. Tell her."

Bess looked at Alma. She could feel her eyes grow wide and she waited in anticipation of what Alma was about to say. Alma leaned in, elbows firmly planted on the table and a big grin spread across her face.

"I'm engaged!" Alma announced and she giggled a little after speaking.

Bess could feel her cards slip through her fingers but she managed to catch them before they hit the table. She felt like someone had just pushed the air right out of her stomach. The news was a complete surprise. After a few seconds to process the news, Bess finally managed to smile at Alma.

"Oh, Alma, I'm so happy for you," Bess said and she reached over and gently gave Alma's hand a squeeze.

"I knew you would be." Alma beamed. "I'm so excited."

"I didn't know you were dating anyone," Bess confessed.

"This has been in the works for quite some time," Rose stated. "Right, Alma?"

Alma simply grinned.

"So where did you two meet?" Bess asked.

"Well, I met Paul last month at a lecture I attended," Alma recalled. "We talked and found that we had a mutual love for the TV show *Perry Mason.* Do you ladies remember *Perry Mason,* the show with Raymond Burr?"

"Oh, yes." Rose nodded. "That was back when TV was good."

"Not like the crap that's on today," Flo cracked. "Now it's just nude and crude, if you ask me."

"Raymond Burr was very handsome back then," Bess nodded.

"Well, Paul and I both love mysteries," Alma explained. "One evening, he came to my room and we flipped on the TV. That's when we found reruns of *Perry Mason* to watch in the evenings. That's when we started spending more time together....all because of *Perry Mason.*"

"Having company in the evening is such a pleasure," Bess said.

"It is." Alma nodded. "Even when the show would end and Paul would start to leave, he'd linger in the doorway with me and we'd just talk. After a while, it occurred to me how much I enjoyed Paul's company. When he was around, I was happy. When he wasn't around, I started to think about when I'd see him again. Then one evening, after an episode of *Perry Mason*, he told me how much he missed me when he got back to his room. It was so sweet. A few episodes later, we decided that since we missed each other so...we should get married."

Bess could feel her mouth slowly drop open the longer she listened to Alma describe how quickly she'd made her decision to get married. Bess knew that Alma was a hopeless romantic by nature. She also knew Alma had been widowed for many years and missed having love in her life. The more she said, the more Bess hoped that this was a decision made with both heart and mind.

Alma and her impending nuptials were the primary focus of conversation for the rest of the Bridge Club meeting. Bess could sense that an impending wedding was a happier topic to discuss than her brother's funeral. Details were given and laughter filled the air while cards were played out on the table.

After many hands of bridge were played, and the hours passed, it was time for everyone to go their separate ways. First Flo ducked out, complaining about having to go for a doctor's appointment for a flu shot. Next, Alma left, grinning from ear to ear about meeting Paul for a walk outside. Only Rose lingered in the Game Room, helping Bess to clean up the cards and push in the chairs around the table.

"So what do you think?' Rose asked.

"About what?' Bess replied.

"What do you think about Alma's news?" Rose asked, and she stepped closer to Bess in anticipation of her answer.

"I think…it's nice," Bess smiled.

"You're not worried?" Rose asked. "She certainly agreed to marry him pretty quickly. Maybe you should do something about it, Bess. I think you should follow that Paul fella around. Find out if he has any secrets he's keeping from Alma."

"I trust Alma," Bess replied.

"I do too," Rose sighed. "I just don't trust him. You know Alma as well as I do. She's got a good heart. Someone could take advantage of a hopeless romantic like her."

Bess slipped the playing cards back into the box and put them on a shelf with an assortment of games.

"I agree that Alma's engagement may have come about very quickly," Bess said. "Sometimes love happens that way, Rose. Did he say or do something to lead you to believe he's taking advantage of her?"

"No," Rose replied. "I've never met him. I'm just afraid for Alma. You know how she tends to focus on the stars when her feet aren't planted firmly on the ground. Besides, you're better at spying on people than me."

"I'm not going to look for a reason to make a friend unhappy," Bess said. She turned around and looked at Rose, who was standing in the doorway with her arms folded. "What Alma does is her business, Rose. Is that why you brought the topic up at the table? Were you hoping I'd investigate and find out something terrible about the man she loves?"

"Well, the thought did cross my mine," Rose sighed and she nervously ran her one hand over her tightly permed white hair.

"Really, Rose," Bess scolded and she could feel her eyebrows lower. "I'm not some wind up toy. You can't just turn me on and expect me to find out bad things about people. There's a fine line between being nosey and being curious about someone based on clues. Now this is Alma's decision…we have to respect that."

"I know you're right." Rose sighed and nervously rubbed her forehead after she spoke, "I just don't want her to get hurt."

Rose's eyes narrowed and her face grew beat red. Clearly, Rose was hoping for help but Bess was still emotionally drained from her trip.

"I'm sorry," Bess said. "I still have a lot on my mind with my brother's death. I'm afraid I can't help you with this, Rose."

Rose's face grew red. She stared at Bess for a few seconds, then turned and walked away. Bess looked down at the table where she and her friends had just been seated. She thought about how good it felt being able to hear their voices and their laughter again. There was something nice about sharing time with people you loved. It was a love built from trust. Bess didn't want to lose that trust by spying on a friend.

Chapter 7: THE SENTIMENTS OF PIE

When she walked home from her Bridge Club meeting, Bess couldn't help but smile. It was the first time in weeks she had something pleasant to think about. Like summer weather in October, Alma's news was the kind of surprise that easily summoned a smile to Bess's lips. It was also the kind of thing that took her mind off her grief and her guilt.

"A hopeless romantic deserves some romance," Bess told herself.

When she got home, she found a note on the kitchen counter.

"At my Investment Club meeting. Be home for lunch. Chet," she read aloud.

She smiled at the message and the thought that his back was feeling good enough to drive himself to the main building for a meeting. She also grinned at the revelation that she had some alone time to work on her garden. She quickly stepped into her garage and collected her gardening glove, a trowel, and a pad to kneel on before heading into the backyard. She smiled at the sight of the two gardens that awaited her attention.

After her trip to California and back, Bess found that her gardening was one thing she could do to help take her mind off the death of her brother. Even though she'd only been back for just a few days, she was still catching up with weeds to be pulled and plants to be watered. When she stepped to the edge of her gardens, she stood with her hands on her hips, surveyed her plants and thought about what needed her attention. With a warm sun burning overhead, Bess looked forward to an afternoon of working on clearing out the dead growth and seeing what was still in bloom. The first frost of the season had yet to arrive, which meant there were still a few things in her garden that were thriving. Just as she was about to grab hold of the first weed to pull, she heard a voice say,

"Hello, Bess."

Bess looked up and found Connie Ocker, a neighbor, walking from her backyard and heading right for Bess's yard. Bess glanced over to her at her gardens, casting a loving smile to her neglected plants, then turned back to her visitor. It appeared that her plants would have to wait a little longer for some nurturing.

"Good morning, Connie." Bess smiled.

"I was talking to Alma Crisp and she told me about your brother," Connie began. Her head tipped down to a small pie she was carrying. "I'm so sorry for your loss, Bess. I made a pumpkin pie for you and Chet. I know it's not much, but when I feel down, a good slice of pumpkin pie always picks my spirits up."

"Thank you, Connie," Bess said and smiled, taking the pie. "That really was very kind of you. Chet and I will both enjoy it."

"It's the least I could do," Connie stated. "Was it an older brother or a younger brother who passed away?"

"A younger brother," Bess said.

"Oh, dear," Connie sighed. "I really am so sorry."

"Thank you," Bess said and her eyes turned to Connie's yard. "So have you cleaned out your garden yet?"

"Not yet," Connie answered. "I've been putting off my garden work. I have lots of things going on these days. Today I'm getting my pumpkin ready for the pumpkin parade."

"The what?" Bess asked.

"The pumpkin parade," Connie replied. "Are you doing it?"

"Yes, we are," Chet's voice spoke up from behind. Bess quickly turned to see her husband stepping out the house and into the yard.

"How was your meeting?" Bess asked and she stepped back and gave him a quick kiss on the cheek.

"Always informative…but I'm afraid I'm still not making us any million dollar investments," Chet laughed.

"And how's your back this morning?" Bess asked. "Feeling any better?"

"It's about the same," Chet sighed.

"Chet has had sciatic nerve problems for weeks," Bess explained to Connie. "We haven't been able to attend our Waltzing Club meetings for quite some time. Isn't that right, dear?"

"I'm afraid that's true," Chet sighed. "I do love dancing, but the doctor says there's simply nothing I can do but rest and wait for my body to heal."

"That's a shame," Connie nodded. A smile crept across her face. "Bess and I were just talking about the pumpkin parade. I can't believe your wife doesn't know about it."

"She's been out of town the last couple weeks," Chet explained. "She's been pretty busy catching up with friends and all."

"It takes time to get caught up with everything after a trip," Connie said with a smile.

"So when were you going to tell me about this parade?" Bess asked, turning to Chet.

"I'll tell you about it later," Chet answered.

Bess found it curious that Chet was so secretive about the whole thing.

"You know, Bess, I lost a younger brother," Connie said, and she stepped forward and took Bess's hand in her own. "I lost him in a car accident when he was in college. It was many years ago. As the oldest in the family, I can still remember how I felt the day he died. You can't help but feel a sense of guilt when you lose a younger sibling. I think that comes from growing up and being told by parents to watch out for a younger brother or sister. A younger sibling dying first is like…breaking a vow we make as children. A vow we take to protect and look out for our younger siblings. It makes grief that much harder for an older brother or sister."

"You have no idea," Bess quietly answered, her eyes glancing out to her garden.

"Try not to let that guilt eat you up," Connie advised and she pointed to her pie.

"Pumpkin pie tastes better than guilt."

Bess smiled politely. She could relate to what Connie said about older siblings losing younger siblings and the guilt that came with it. However, Bess also harbored a darker guilt that she kept to herself. It was the kind of guilt she didn't speak of to anyone, not even Chet. She hoped that time, and a slice of pumpkin pie, was all she would need to work through the feelings that still lingered from her brother's death.

Chapter 8: RESPONSIBILITY

It was well past midnight and Bess was unable to sleep. Despite the late hour, and her husband quietly slumbering beside her, Bess was wide-awake. Her mind was racing through the memories from the day of the funeral. Accompanying her memories was the clarity of heartache she felt from burying her brother.

When she closed her eyes to sleep, images of the funeral kept flickering in her mind...faces crying...words spoken out of remorse. She could easily recall her conversation with Connie about the guilt that came with being an older sister. She even had the briefest of dreams about a pumpkin pie, which probably meant she'd had one too many slices after dinner.

Finally, Bess gave up trying to sleep. She swung her legs out from under the sheet, turned and managed to tuck her feet into her slippers without waking Chet. She put on her robe, then lingered at her dresser where she grabbed two things from a drawer.

Shuffling out to the living room, she walked over to the front door, opened it and stepped outside. Leaving the comfort of her air-conditioned home, the autumn air was still warm and muggy despite the late hour. It smothered Bess with a warm embrace and for a moment she forgot what season it was. In the distance, a honey-colored moon lingered just above her neighbor's roof. Occasionally, the soft call of crickets filled the silence. Bess settled into a chair on her front porch and pulled out the two things she'd grabbed from her dresser. She squinted at the items in the moonlight.

One item was a lighter, which she placed on a small table next to her chair. The second item was a pack of cigarettes. She tapped one cigarette out of the pack and turned it in her hand. She held the cigarette between her thumb and index finger and sniffed it. Her eyes looked up to the stars in the sky and she thought about her brother.

"One last time, Donald," Bess whispered.

She picked up the lighter, flicked it and watched a small plum-shaped flame glow in front of her face. She slipped the cigarette between her lips, held the flame close and inhaled. A warm sensation filled her lungs. She put the lighter down while smoke curled around her face. She blew smoke into the air and quietly reflected on what she was doing.

"Bess?" a voice asked.

She looked to see Chet standing in the doorway. She could tell by the expression on his face, and his disheveled hair, that he was half-awake. She could also tell he was surprised by what he was looking at.

"It's after midnight," Chet said, stepping out the front door. He tightened the sash on his navy blue robe and pushed his white hair to the side. "What are you doing up? And you're out here…smoking? I didn't even know you smoked. Is this some dirty little habit you've been hiding from me?"

"No, no," Bess sighed and she carefully gestured with the cigarette in one hand. "Curiosity is my only secret habit, dear. You already know about that."

"Then what is this?" Chet asked and he dragged a chair across the porch and sat down beside Bess. He looked out to the street to see if any neighbor's lights were on in their homes. When it appeared they were the only two people on Dogwood Lane awake, Chet leaned closer to Bess. "Tell me why you're out here in the middle of the night smoking."

"It's...because of Donald," Bess sighed.

"Donald?" Chet asked.

Bess nodded, tucked the cigarette between her lips and blew out some more smoke.

"When I was a girl," Bess began pulling the cigarette from her lips, "Donald and I would go to the movies a lot. Of course, I wanted to be sophisticated like the actresses I'd see on screen. They always smoked and they always seemed to attract the good-looking guys. Being in high school, I guess I wanted to attract some handsome boys, too. So I had this idea to start smoking. Of course, I didn't tell my parents about it."

"Where did you get the cigarettes?" Chet asked.

"I snuck a few from the janitor's office when I was in school," Bess explained. "We had one janitor in our school and he was always busy. Sneaking into his office for a cigarette or two was easy. Then, after school, I'd go off to a nearby field and practice smoking before I'd go home. I'd practice how to hold the cigarette, how to light it, and how to hold it when I spoke. Being sophisticated took some practice. And that's when it happened."

"What happened?" Chet asked.

"One day Donald followed me after school and caught me smoking in the field," Bess recalled.

"How old was Donald back when all this happened?" Chet asked.

"He had just started high school and I was about to finish," Bess explained. "I can remember it like it was yesterday, Chet. I can still see him standing in that field telling me how he wanted to try a cigarette because I was smoking one. Being a big sister, I told him he was too young. Then he threatened to tell our parents, so I found myself being forced to agree to his request."

"Smart boy, bribing you like that," Chet mumbled.

"Yes, Donald was smart," Bess sighed and she flicked some cigarette ash to the ground. "So I showed him how to light it, how to hold it, and when to breathe in and out. He coughed a good bit the first few times…but he got the hang of it. From then on, whenever I'd steal a cigarette from the janitor's room we'd share it in the field. We swore we'd never tell our parents and we kept that promise."

"That doesn't surprise me," Chet said. "You've always been discrete, Bess."

"Years later," Bess continued, "when I was married, I quit smoking because I was pregnant with Samantha. I just thought it would be a good thing to do. Once she was born it just seemed silly to have all that smoke around a baby. It was hard to stop but I did it. I just never imagined…that because of that one day after school, that one time he caught me in that field…Donald would become a lifelong smoker. I feel like…"

Bess grew silent and took another drag of her cigarette.

"You feel like what?" Chet asked.

"I feel like I killed him," Bess replied.

She grew silent again, and stared down at the dim orange ember at the tip of the cigarette.

"You didn't know you were starting him down that path back then," Chet suggested. "You were just a child."

"I put him on that path," Bess sighed. She stared out at the darkness and she slowly nodded to nothing in particular. "I taught him that dirty little habit. It's my fault he's dead, Chet. That's just how I feel about what happened to Donald."

With those words she took another drag on her cigarette, flicked some more ashes into the air and winced. She looked at Chet and raised the cigarette in the air.

"When I was visiting out there, I found this pack of cigarettes in the nightstand of Donald's home," Bess explained. "I took it when no one was looking and brought it all the way back from California. This was the brand he liked. The way it smelled when I held it to my nose just reminded me of how Donald smelled."

"I had no idea one brand could be different than another," Chet said.

"They are," Bess nodded. "Since Donald liked this particular brand so much...I thought I'd try one. I wanted to know if it was this brand of cigarette that made it so hard for him to quit."

"So that's why you're out here?" Chet asked.

"Yes," Bess replied. "You know it's my nature to be curious about things."

"And after trying it," Chet began, "do you have your answer?"

Bess pulled the cigarette to her face and looked at it. She leaned forward in her chair and rested her elbows on her knees. She turned the cigarette in her hand, the orange glow filling her eyes. The smoke spiraled up into the darkness. Then, without warning, Bess simply tossed the cigarette down on the cement and watched the small bright ember burn.

"I don't think this cigarette is all that special," Bess sighed. She leaned back in her chair. "I wish Donald would have felt the same way."

"I wish he would have, too," Chet replied.

Together Bess and Chet sat quietly, looking out at the stars, the darkness, and the full honey-colored moon that crested high in the sky. After a few minutes, the orange glow from the cigarette had vanished. The smell of cigarette smoke subsided. Bess looked down at the darkness and knew that Donald's last vice was gone.

While the cigarette lost its glow and the smoke had vanished, the guilt over his death did not vanish into the darkness.

Chapter 9: THE PENSIVE PRIEST

One of the benefits of living a long life is learning how to cope with the death of loved ones. From parents, to a husband to a premature child, Bess had had her share of losses in her life. Each time she lost someone, Bess leaned on the church and her faith for strength. Since returning from her trip to California, Bess began to realize her grief and her guilt was too much for her to deal with on her own. She needed to rely on her faith again. Fortunately, the Honey Hills Center was able to help.

While Honey Hills was a non-denominational retirement home, it embraced Christianity and all of its beliefs in heaven and God. As such, there was a wide range of services and numerous local church leaders who came to visit throughout the week to meet the spiritual needs of residents. Bess attended church every Sunday, but she also went to services for residents of other denominations as well. Her curious nature led her not just to mysteries, but to get different perspectives on how people knew God through how they worshipped.

Because she attended a variety of services, she also had the opportunity to get to know most of the church leaders who came to lead the services. She'd even spotted a few of them walking around the hallways to visit parishioners who were residents. While she enjoyed chatting with some of the church leaders, her favorite one to talk to was Father Francis Mahoney.

On a typical day, Father Mahoney was a busy man when he visited Honey Hills. A few mornings a week, he came to visit and offered communion to the

Catholics who were residents. Father Mahoney was easy to spot, moving from one room to the next with a quick step, a ready smile, and a sense of urgency in every stride he took. Because of the speed with which he moved through the halls, Bess found it a bit challenging to even engage Father Mahoney in a discussion. From the moment he set foot in the retirement home, he walked fast, checked his watch often, and never lingered in one place for very long. In every way, Father Mahoney appeared to be a man who lived life on a tight schedule. Bess had tried to seek him out once or twice since her return. Yet, every time she saw him, her eye for curious behaviors would override her wounded heart. When she saw Father Mahoney, he didn't appear to be the same man she knew before her trip.

Rather than charging down hallways with reckless abandon, Bess noticed how Father Mahoney's strides were more measured and less rushed. She also noticed that he wasn't nervously checking his watch when he moved from one room to the next. Instead, she found him taking more time to talk to residents, rather than popping in and out of their rooms the way a butterfly would visit a flower. Bess found it to be a remarkable transformation for a man who had spent so many days focused on his tight schedule.

One morning, Bess was on her way to play bridge with her friends when she spotted Father Mahoney standing by the entrance to the main building. He was meandering around a garden just outside the entrance. She found her steps slowing down and her eyes began to really study him. She stopped by the doors and couldn't help but let her eyes soak up the details around this man.

With bright vibrant fall perennials spread before him, he stood with his arms tucked behind his back, his hands folded together, his eyes fixed on the bright colors that sprouted up from the ground and filled the garden.

Some people were leaving the main building and Bess stepped to the side so they could pass. Her eyes flicked back to her subject, who was still staring at the garden. She guessed that Father Mahoney's mind was occupied with weighty thoughts, which was not all that unusual for a man of the church. However, the expression on his face truly did not reflect the pleasant feelings that a garden typically brings forth. The expression, Bess thought, also didn't reflect a man occupied with peaceful thoughts. With that last clue, Bess checked her watch and stepped inside to find her friends.

When she arrived at the game room, the other three members of her Bridge Club were in attendance and greeted her with smiles. A few comments were made about her tardiness, which Bess ignored. Once the first bridge game of the morning began, Bess began to unburden herself.

She started to talk about her brother, his cigarette habit, and the embarrassment of being caught smoking by Chet. She also began to talk about her guilt for her brother's death. She confessed, much to the surprise of her friends, that she had once been a smoker and had gotten her little brother hooked on the habit. Despite their kind words, Bess couldn't shake the notion that she was responsible for his death.

"He was a grown man, Bess," Rose commented. "You can't put yourself in charge of him for a lifetime. He made his choices, Bess."

"I agree," Alma said. "He was his own man. He chose to keep smoking."

Bess quietly nodded at the words, but really said nothing to indicate she agreed with the sentiment being shared at the table. Bess's silence drew the attention of Rose, who was sitting across the table. She lowered her cards and looked at Bess.

"Maybe you should talk to Father Mahoney," Rose suggested. "He's always in here and he's always willing to sit and listen to our problems. I know he listens to mine when I feel down and I'm not even Catholic. He's a good man, in my opinion."

"He certainly is," Bess said, lowering her cards a bit. "You know, I actually thought about doing that. I even spotted him on my way in here this morning. Do any of you see him?"

"All the residents see him," Flo replied. "He's impossible to miss on a Wednesday. He's in the halls, he's in the rooms, sometimes he even steps into the Dining Hall to smile and shake hands with people. He's everywhere."

"That's not what I mean," Bess said and she shook her head. "I mean does he come into any of your rooms? Does he give any of you communion or meet with you? It's just that...what I feel...I'd rather talk to him in a private rather than in the hallway where residents can hear what I say. I don't think he'd make a special visit to my house. He only comes to the main building."

"I'll see him tomorrow," Flo quickly responded. "He's coming to give me communion in my room. You're more than welcome to come and talk to him, Bess."

"Flo?" Alma said and she lowered her cards "I didn't know you were Catholic?"

"It's not a crime," Flo answered.

"I didn't mean it that way," Alma said and she began to nervously tap her cards on the table. "No, no, Flo...it's just that..."

"Just what?" Flo asked.

"It's just that you always talk about working in the casinos in Atlantic City. I just never thought that..." Alma tried to explain.

"That I went to church?" Flo laughed and her eyes narrowed. "They have Catholic churches in Atlantic City, Alma. The city isn't just full of casinos."

Alma grew silent and her eyes quickly retreated to the safety of her cards.

"As I was saying, Bess, you're welcome to come to my room if you want to talk to him about your brother's death," Flo mumbled.

"Thank you," Bess sighed. She looked around the table. "What does he do when he visits you?"

"Sometimes he'll read a scripture and say a prayer. Mainly he gives me communion and does a blessing. It's the same thing every Wednesday," Flo said very matter-of-factly.

"I see. Thank you, Flo, for that invitation. I think I'll take you up on it," Bess said. She looked around the table. "Ladies, being away from this place for a few weeks has given me a new perspective on Father Mahoney. Since I've been back I've observed him to be a little slower in getting around. Have any of you noticed that?"

"We all slow down as we get older," Rose pointed out, and she shrugged her shoulders to emphasize her point. "He's not a young man, Bess. He's getting older like the rest of us."

"I don't think this is about age," Bess stated. "I think this is about something else. He walks slower, he stops and chats to residents, he stares at the garden out by the main entrance...that's not the Father Mahoney I remember. He used to walk through this place in record time then hop back in his car and take off. He never stopped to look at the garden. He never spent more than two minutes in a room. What would cause a person to change like that? That, ladies, is the question that has been on my mind this morning."

"So how do you intend on finding an answer?" Alma asked.

"Thanks to Flo's invitation…I have an idea," Bess replied and she smiled across the table at Flo.

"I don't like the sound of that," Flo mumbled.

Chapter 10: PURSUING A PRIEST

The next morning, Bess found herself waking to an alarm clock. It was not the normal way for her to start her morning. On occasion, she'd set it for doctor appointments, but, on the whole, alarms really weren't used to wake up retired people. She sat up in bed and quickly slammed her hand down on the clock, silencing the buzzer. She checked to see if Chet was still asleep, then reached over to her nightstand for her glasses.

She slipped out of bed, wincing at the pain from her one arthritic knee, before tucking her feet into her slippers. She ducked into the bathroom to change, fix her hair and brush her teeth. A few minutes later, she headed to the kitchen, her knee beginning to feel less painful, and grabbed a muffin for breakfast.

When she finished, Bess grabbed a lightweight coat, stepped out into the morning sun and began the walk from her house on Dogwood Lane to the main building of the Honey Hills Center. With each step, the details of the morning unfurled before her: the gentle calls of a distant bird, the soft breezes that stirred the colorful leaves on the limbs, the golden sunlight that was still warm on her face despite the autumn season. In the distance, a corn field that looked more lush and green than withered and brown.

When she arrived at the main building, Bess took a familiar route of turns through certain hallways before stopping in front of the door to Flo Morgenstern's room. Bess curled her fingers into a fist and knocked. The door opened and Flo appeared with a typical grimace on her face. Rather than greeting Bess with a friendly morning salutation, Flo simply opened the door and waved for her to come in.

"Come in," she mumbled

"Has he been here yet?" Bess asked, stepping inside.

"No," Flo snapped. She waved a finger in the air towards Bess. "Now when he does come, please remember, he's here to visit me. Let me get communion and a blessing from Father Mahoney before you start talking to him."

"I promise to wait my turn," Bess nodded.

Flo sat down in one chair. Bess sat beside her in another and for the next few minutes, both ladies observed the silence that settled between them. Some voices could be heard in the hallway, growing stronger before fading away. Flo sat with her hands on her lap, eyes fixed on the doorway, her lips pressed together in anticipation of speaking with Father Mahoney. The longer they waited, the more uncomfortable Bess began to feel with the silence. Finally, she turned to Flo and thought of something to say.

"Is that new lipstick you're wearing?" Bess asked, pointing in Flo's direction.

"No," Flo answered.

"It looks more lavender than red to me," Bess observed. "I'm always used to seeing you wear red lipstick."

"This *is* red," Flo stated. "Same color I always wear."

"Well, it looks lavender to me," Bess said.

"It's the same lipstick I've worn all year, Bess. If you think this is lavender, you better get your eyes checked," Flo grumbled.

Once again silence filled the room. While Bess was used to Flo's edge and sarcasm, she found the silence more uncomfortable than before. Seconds felt like minutes. Soon Bess found her eyes being drawn to the doorway. Together, both ladies sat, staring at the door with very little expression on their faces. Suddenly, there was a knock on the door. The tension in the air was gone. Both ladies smiled.

"Come in!" Flo called out.

The door opened to reveal Father Mahoney. An older man, with snow white hair and glasses, he smiled at Flo and Bess when he entered the room.

"Good morning, Flo," Father Mahoney said. "I see you have some company this morning. Should I come back a little later?"

"No, no," Flo said, struggling to pull herself out of her chair. She waved her hand towards Bess. "This is my friend, Bess Bullock. She's here for a short visit. Please stay, Father."

"Yes," Bess nodded, "please join us."

"I believe your friend and I have met before....haven't we?" Father Mahoney grinned as he stepped into the room.

"We've passed each other in the hallways," Bess nodded. "I think we even spoke once or twice."

"I always remember a face," Father Mahoney smiled and he snapped his fingers after speaking. He ran his hand over his short white hair like he was brushing away some dust and his smile faded. "Names I have trouble with...but faces I remember."

"I'm the same way," Bess nodded in an attempt to win some trust by pointing out a mutual quality they shared. "I must say, Father, for the number of people you see in our retirement home, not to mention your church, I'd imagine that you have a lot of faces to memorize as a priest."

"I do see a lot of faces in a week's time," he sighed and his eyes drifted to his shoes. "Though, I'm sorry to say, that number is shrinking."

"Oh, dear," Bess said and she rubbed her chin with her hand. "I'd suppose at a retirement home, residents are bound to pass away."

That," he said, "and a number of my parishioners who have chosen to move away from my church."

"Why is that?' Bess asked.

"Many reasons," Father Mahoney sighed. "Soon...I'm afraid I will be joining them. Soon I'll be one of those faces who is moving on to greener pastures."

"Father?" Flo finally spoke. "What are you saying? Are you going somewhere?"

"I've been meaning to tell you," Father Mahoney began and then his eyes looked down at the floor and he cleared his throat. "I've been meaning to tell a lot of people, Flo, but it's been difficult to do. You see, the church has seen fit to send me to another city."

Bess looked at Flo, who had covered her mouth with her hand upon hearing the news.

"I'm so sorry to hear that," Bess said.

"There are a lot of people around here I will miss," Father Mahoney said. He turned his eyes to Flo and smiled. "People like you, Flo."

"But why, Father?' Flo asked. "You've been here for years. Why are you leaving?"

"Like I was telling your friend...the church's numbers have been on the decline the last few years," he explained. "Of course, since you live at Honey Hills, Flo, you don't know what goes on at our church anymore. However, I don't look at it as being the opportunity for an end. I like to think of it as a chance for a new beginning."

Flo was clearly affected by the news. She sat back in her chair and rubbed her forehead the same way she would after losing in a game of bridge or bingo. Bess turned back to Father Mahoney and decided to pose one more question.

"When did you find out that they were moving you?" Bess asked.

"I was contacted a few weeks ago," he answered.

The comment caused Bess to crack a small smile, which she quickly tried to contain.

She wasn't happy about his departure. Yet, his reply simply confirmed her observations about his behavior. Before she'd left for California, he was an active, quick walking priest, eager to see everyone and leave. Upon her return, he'd been transformed into a slower-paced man. However, his pace was not a reflection of his old age. The news that he would be leaving the ones he loved in this retirement home was what had transformed him into a slower more thoughtful visitor. He was no longer simply keeping appointments. Now he was savoring his final days, knowing that his time at Honey Hills was coming to a close.

"I'd imagine it will be hard for you to leave," Bess said.

"I've been here for twelve years," Father Mahoney replied. "A lot of good relationships have been formed over that time…a lot of smiling faces that I'll take with me." He paused and turned to Flo.

"Faces like yours, Flo," he said in a soft voice. "I've always enjoyed my visits with you. We've had many good conversations about life and I'll miss that."

Bess could see Flo's chin tremble just a bit, and she looked away as Father Mahoney sat down on the edge of her bed. He opened his Bible and began to read to Bess and Flo. He also offered a prayer for both of them to continue to have good health. Then he gave Flo communion and offered both ladies a blessing.

Bess took it all in. She watched him speak with a slow deliberate rhythm. He was never rushed and answered every question Flo asked. He eased every concern. He smiled at all the right times. He was patient and kind from the first word he spoke to the moment he stood up and told Flo to have a good day. Flo clearly looked happy about the visit. Bess didn't want to dampen the happy mood Flo was in by bringing up her brother's death. Instead, she followed Father Mahoney into the hallway. Once in the hall, Bess quickly stepped in front of him before he went to another room.

"Father," Bess began. "May I speak with you for a moment?"

"Of course," he answered.

Bess looked around. Standing in the hallway was the last place she wanted to broach the subject of her grief, but it would appear this was where she'd have to do it.

"My brother passed away from cancer a few weeks ago," Bess began. She looked down and shook her head slightly. She took a deep breath to try to calm her nerves before looking back at the priest. "I...I feel responsible for his death."

"Were you involved in the death in some way?" he asked.

"No...not exactly," Bess said and she folded her arms at her waist. "You see, I got him started on cigarettes quite by accident. It happened a long time ago. When I think back on the day that I gave him that first cigarette...I just never thought it would be the reason he would die as an older man."

"And when did this happen?" Father Mahoney asked.

"We were children. We were barely teenagers," Bess recalled. "We went to the movies a lot and I thought smoking looked glamorous. That's why I wanted to try it. My brother wanted to do it because I was doing it. Eventually, I stopped when I had my daughter. Unfortunately, my brother never did. He died of cancer last month. I feel so guilty for what I've done, Father. How can I cope with this guilt?"

Bess looked away from the priest and she could feel her eyes well up. She sniffed and wiped the corner of one eye with the back of her hand.

"God can forgive you," Father Mahoney said. "However, before you can feel God's forgiveness, you really must forgive yourself. You were a child and you made a child's mistake. None of us can go through life carrying the mistakes we make as children. If we placed every sin we ever committed into a bucket and carried it around for the rest of our days, it would be a very heavy bucket to bear...don't you think?"

"Yes it would, Father," Bess said.

"Would your brother want this?" Father Mahoney continued. "Would he want you to bear that burden from your childhood? Would he want you to be riddled with guilt over his addiction to cigarettes? Would he want tears or smiles?"

"My brother was always a happy person," Bess quietly answered.

"As I said," Father Mahoney smiled, "the Lord always forgives us for our sins. Forgive yourself, Mrs. Bullock. That is your penance."

Chapter 11: A CURIOSITY IN FALL

"It's time to put the colors of summer away."

Bess spoke these words to herself more than once as the days tumbled by and it became more apparent that the autumn season was clearly settling in. Despite the fact that the trees in her neighborhood were being magically transformed into bright bouquets of crimson, gold, and peach, it did nothing to stir her enthusiasm for the season. She knew the colors would soon fade. The leaves would turn brown. The air would grow colder. While she appreciated autumn's flare, she loved the summer season and despised the fall for taking it away.

As the days moved deeper into October, Bess could detect the subtle changes to her neighborhood. She took note to how the angle of the sun was getting lower in the sky. How the morning sun was looking more buttery-yellow than white. How the shadows were growing longer and darker. How her neighbors had removed hanging baskets from their porches and replaced them with pots filled with crimson, orange and yellow mums. On the occasions she found herself admiring a bright yellow tree, a dry brown leaf would tumble by to remind her that the beauty wouldn't last. Colder days were coming. More importantly to Bess, the number of days she had left to work in her beloved gardens were dwindling.

Despite what the calendar told her, Bess continued to maintain her routine. She took her morning walks. She weeded out dry brush from her gardens. She even managed to eat lunch a few times on her back porch.

While the sun was still warm enough to enjoy the outdoors, Bess was well aware that the colors of summer were fading away.

One morning, while stepping out on her front porch to retrieve the newspaper, Bess found her eyes quickly drawn to something out of place on her porch. She tied her robe closed, took a few steps out on her porch and stopped. She stared at a large curious thing sitting just a few feet from her front door. Her eyes narrowed and her mind raced at what she was looking at.

"Oh my," Bess managed to say to the crisp morning air.

There on her front porch was a bright orange splash of color. A pumpkin, larger than she'd ever seen, had magically appeared on her porch. Bess stepped over to the pumpkin to give it a closer inspection. She drew in her breath when she saw that the pumpkin was so big it actually went up to her knees. She reached down and ran her hand over its smooth orange surface.

"Where did you come from?" Bess asked the pumpkin. "Always nice to have a visitor, but you should have called first."

"Talking to a pumpkin?" Chet asked, stepping into the doorway with a wide grin on his face. He had a mug of coffee in his hand and gestured with it like he was about to give a toast. "Really, Bess, chatting with a pumpkin will only give the neighbors something to gossip about."

"Very funny," Bess chuckled. She turned and pointed at the pumpkin. "I came out for the newspaper and…this is what I found. Look at the size of it, Chet. It's huge!"

"And the paper?" Chet asked while in between sips of coffee. "Did you find it?"

Bess found his question and demeanor curious. Was he really that concerned about a newspaper? Was he really that disinterested in this obvious mystery?

"Maybe it's under the pumpkin," Bess said, waving her finger at it.

"I hope not," Chet laughed. "With my sore back…that would be a problem."

"Chet," Bess began and her head tilted to one side, "aren't you at all curious about where this pumpkin came from? I mean, a pumpkin this size just doesn't show up on a porch every day."

"I'll tell you a secret," Chet said and he stepped closer to Bess. A small grin appeared on his face as if he were a school boy about to convey a secret. "I know exactly where this pumpkin came from."

"You do?" Bess asked, a bit confused.

"Yes," Chet nodded. "You see, Bess, this is all about that Pumpkin Parade. Do you remember talking to Connie about it?"

"I do," Bess quickly replied.

"Well the idea is that all the residents in our neighborhood are going to decorate a pumpkin and place it on their porch," Chet explained. "Then, in about a week or so, they're going to bring residents over from the main building to see all the pumpkins on display. We even get to vote for our favorite pumpkins. I think the idea was to give everyone a reason to get outside one last time before the weather gets cold."

"It appears to me that we may have the largest pumpkin," Bess observed, glancing at her neighbors' homes. "Where did you find one so big, Chet?"

"I actually called a few of the farms around here," Chet explained. "I managed to locate one farmer who said he was growing pumpkins. I told him I wanted the biggest pumpkin he had and that money was no option.

When I agreed to his price, he offered to deliver the pumpkin this morning."

"Really, Chet?" Bess laughed, glancing back at the pumpkin. "Now why would you spend good money on something like this?"

"Because I wanted to make our pumpkin the best," Chet replied with a shrug of his shoulders. "I want to win the prize for best pumpkin."

"Well, now this sounds more like a competition than a parade," Bess mumbled.

"First prize is a gift card to that restaurant in town, the one we like...Greta's Kitchen. You know I like the soup there," Chet announced in an effort to justify his position.

"First prize is...dinner?" Bess laughed. "Chet, did it ever occur to you that the money you paid for that pumpkin might have been more than enough for both of us to eat there?"

"You know me, Bess," Chet began and his relaxed blue eyes grew just a little wider. "When I do something, dear, I do it right. Whether it's dancing with our Waltzing Club, or picking stocks with the members of my Investment Club, I want to be the best at what I do. Yes, I paid for that pumpkin so I could win a free meal at a local restaurant, but that's how I am. I've always been very competitive about things."

Bess couldn't help but smile. While her husband of just over a year was soft spoken and modest about many things, there apparently burned a fire in him that Bess didn't know existed. There was a competitive fire that quietly simmered in the body of this retired contract lawyer. She always saw the man who enjoyed dancing, liked to laugh and was pretty easy going about things. She didn't really see the side of him that wanted to win.

"Well," Bess said, resting her hands on her slender hips. "What are we going to do with this, Chet? It looks like some of our neighbors have decorated their pumpkins. Perhaps I could simply hollow it out first. It's just…so big. I've never carved a pumpkin this big before."

"Whatever you think," Chet said.

Bess turned and looked her neighborhood. The sky was clear and blue and filling with sunlight.

"It's a nice morning," Bess said, squinting up at the sky. "I think we should work out here and decorate it together. I can't remember the last time you and I worked on a project side by side."

"That sounds like fun," Chet nodded.

"Wait here," Bess instructed and she stepped into the house. A few seconds later she emerged with a large knife and some paper towels. She waved the knife in the direction of the pumpkin.

"Do you know what you're doing?" Chet asked, casting a concerned look at the size of the knife.

"I did this before," Bess began.

"When?" Chet asked.

"Maybe…fifty years ago," Bess giggled.

"So you carved pumpkins as a mother? Something you did for Samantha?" Chet asked.

"Yes," Bess answered. "I learned from my dad. When I was a girl, my father and I used to cut a pumpkin into a fine looking jack-o-lantern."

"Now that's a good thing for a father to teach his daughter," Chet laughed.

"It's been many years since I did this, but I think I'd like to try it again," Bess said, dangling the knife just above the pumpkin. "By the time I'm done, Chet, we'll have the best looking jack-o-lantern on Dogwood Lane. I promise."

"That's nice, sweetheart, except for one thing," Chet said.

"What's that?" Bess asked.

"I was actually going to paint the pumpkin, not turn it into a jack-o-lantern," Chet stated.

"Well I'd like to cut it and get the seeds out," Bess stated, getting close to the pumpkin and raising the knife in the air the way someone would before stabbing an intruder. "Now come here, Chet, and hold this pumpkin still so I can start with the eyes."

Chet watched as Bess began. He was amazed at how skillful she was in being able to carve eyes, nose and a mouth without any type of drawing on the face of the pumpkin. Once the facial features were complete, she cut a hole in the top of the pumpkin. She asked Chet to retrieve two buckets, then filled them with the insides of the pumpkin. When the last of the insides were scooped out, Bess sat back and felt some arthritis surge in her hand.

She rubbed the knuckles and closed her eyes.

"Are you okay?" Chet asked.

"I'm fine," Bess answered. She flexed her hand a few times and the pain subsided.

She turned around and offered a smile to Chet. "I'd say we're off to a good start. Now that we've hollowed it out, lets work on making it scary."

"Sounds good," Chet nodded and he rubbed his chin while she stared down at the pumpkin. "I'll be right back with my paint."

Chet grabbed the bucket in one hand, the knife in the other, and headed into the house. When he came back out Bess was surprised to see what he was holding: spray paint, bright red hair, a small red ball and a funny looking hat.

"Chet," Bess stated. "What are you going to do?"

"I've given it a good deal of thought, Bess, and I think I have a good idea for how to win," Chet grinned.

"And what is that?" Bess asked.

"I thought about how the parade of pumpkins will feature lots of orange pumpkins. After a while, all of those pumpkins will look the same," Chet said, carefully putting his supplies on a table next to the pumpkin.

"Pumpkins are typically orange, so you're right about that," Bess grinned.

"I thought it would be fun to turn this pumpkin into a clown," Chet announced.

"A what?" Bess asked, surprised by his suggestion.

"We can give it some bushy red hair, a hat, spray on some white paint for a face," Chet continued. "I even have a small red ball we can attach for the nose. Clowns make people laugh. Nobody will remember a scary pumpkin because they're so common. A pumpkin dressed like a clown will stand out, Bess. They'll remember it when they vote for their favorite."

"Well, Chet," Bess laughed, choosing her words carefully so as not discourage Chet's enthusiasm. "It seems to me that you've really thought things through."

"I've had a lot of spare time sitting around the house with my bad back," Chet smiled. "So, yes, I did put a lot of thought into it."

"I don't ever recall seeing a clown pumpkin before," Bess stated. "How are we going to do this?"

"I have a plan, but it may take a good bit of time to do," Chet said. "Are you willing to help me, Bess?"

"There's nowhere else I'd rather be," Bess grinned.

Together they remained on the porch for an hour, painting, gluing, and mounting things in such a way that they began to see how their efforts were transforming their pumpkin into something more festive. Soon the red hair was attached, the red nose glued on, a hat positioned, and the project was completed. Chet stepped back and grinned at the finished product positioned at the front of their porch.

"What do you think?" Chet asked, staring down at the decorated pumpkin.

"I have to be honest," Bess began. "If someone walked by our porch...I'm afraid they might think we chopped off the head of some wayward circus clown and left it outside."

She let her eyes roll over the object of their collaborative efforts. A large pumpkin, painted white, with red paint around the holes she cut for eyes. There was a small red ball glued to the nose and red paint around the mouth that Bess had cut. On top, long red curly hair was attached and a bright blue hat was attached to the wig.

"If anyone walks down our street, it will be hard to miss this," Bess said, pointing to the pumpkin. "I'm afraid it won't look very festive for the fall season, Chet. Not even for Halloween."

"Well, I think it looks very jolly," Chet observed. "Clowns are jolly, don't you think?"

"It looks creepy to me, Chet," Bess surmised and she shook her head at the sight.

"'Tis the season for things like this," Chet said and he drew in his breath, wrapped his arm around her waist and pulled her close. "I think it's safe to say we will have the best looking pumpkin for the parade."

Bess simply smiled at her husband's childlike enthusiasm to win this contest. She hoped their clown pumpkin would do the trick. Despite the end result, Bess quite enjoyed spending the afternoon outside working in the sunshine with her husband. The experience gave them something to reflect on over dinner. It also gave Bess something more pleasant to think about when she climbed into bed and drifted off to sleep. For tonight, the guilt in her heart had been replaced with laughter over her husband's childlike enthusiasm.

The next morning, Bess got up early. It was Tuesday morning, which meant she had to dress and head over to the main building for a meeting of her Bridge Club. She quietly slipped out of bed and dressed while Chet snored. He was a notoriously late sleeper which made Bess accustomed to getting up first and dressing to her husband's snores.

She went out to the kitchen and helped herself to a quick bowl of oatmeal and a banana while she considered what she would talk to her friends about. She wanted to remember to thank Flo again for allowing her to meet with Father Mahoney. Bess found his words helpful, but difficult to do. Forgiving herself was something she was struggling with.

A few minutes later, she placed her dirty dishes in the sink, and grabbed her coat before heading out for her morning walk.

The second she cracked open the door, cool autumn air poured in and splashed in her face, sending a chill down to her toes. The temperature surprised Bess. She quickly zipped up her jacket and stepped out to the front porch. She squinted up at the clear blue sky. She closed her eyes and let the warm sunlight strike her face. While the air was cool and fresh, the sun was still warm enough to make her walk a good one. As she was about to step inside to change, she glanced over to the side of the porch to catch a glimpse of Chet's odd looking clown pumpkin.

She looked left. She looked right. She looked left again. She stepped off the porch and glanced around the front yard. She turned her eyes up and down Dogwood

Lane. She turned back to the front porch one more time. Just as it had magically appeared on her porch, Bess was stunned to see that their large pumpkin was gone.

Chapter 12: NEWS OVER CARDS

"Good morning, ladies," Bess began, entering the Game Room. Flo, Rose and Alma were already seated and a deck of cards was being shuffled and cut for the first round. Bess looked around the table at her friends, unzipped her coat, and carefully placed it over the back of her chair.

"It certainly is a cool morning for you to walk over, Bess," Rose observed. "You might want to start wearing a thicker coat. You're not in California anymore."

"It is getting cooler," Alma added. "Maybe Chet should start driving you."

"You both might be right," Bess replied while sitting down. She smiled and decided to offer the riddle that woke her up when she stepped out on her front porch. "Did any of you happen to see a one-hundred pound pumpkin this morning?"

Rose and Alma both laughed at the comment. Flo was too busy shuffling the cards to crack a smile.

"Things always get more interesting when you're here, Bess," Alma chuckled.

"You're right, Alma," Rose said, dealing out cards for the first round of bridge.

"You may think I am joking, but I'm not," Bess replied. "You see, while I was on my trip, my dear husband got it in his head to buy this enormous pumpkin from a local farmer."

"Was it for the Parade of Pumpkins?" Alma asked.

"I'm afraid it was," Bess nodded. "Chet and I took a few hours to carve it and decorate it. It was fun spending time outside and doing something together as a couple. So often I work in my garden by myself. It was fun having someone to work with and talk to about what we were doing."

"The more people around me the better," Alma smiled.

"After a few hours," Bess continued, "we had this lovely looking pumpkin all decorated and ready for that Parade of Pumpkins. Unfortunately, when I went to leave for our meeting this morning, the pumpkin was gone."

Silence met her news. Bess knew that a pumpkin was not something of great value, like a car or a piece of jewelry. Yet, she couldn't help but think about how something so big could have been taken away.

"It took the two of us to move it just a little on the porch," Bess explained. "And Chet, with his bad back, wasn't much help. So the question, ladies, is who would be strong enough to move a hundred-pound pumpkin off of someone's front porch? I, for one, cannot think of any possibilities."

Again, silence followed her statement.

"Ladies," Bess began and she leaned forward and felt the urge to raise her voice. "Are you listening to me?"

"Of course we are," Rose sighed.

"We're trying to play bridge, Bess," Flo snapped. "Enough with the chatter."

"I think I know what happened to your pumpkin," Alma spoke up. "It is fall. Everyone is eating pumpkin pie. I'll bet that someone needed a big pumpkin to fill a lot of orders for pumpkin pies. So they came to your house, saw your pumpkin and sliced it up right there on your porch. I bet they even brought baggies along to cut up the pumpkin and keep the slices. They're probably baking lots of pumpkin pies right now. What do you think, ladies? Have I solved this mystery for Bess?"

"I'm getting a headache," Flo mumbled.

""Thank you for that…suggestion, Alma," Bess smiled. She looked down at her cards and shook her head. "Poor Chet. He was so excited about that pumpkin. I haven't even told him yet, but he may discover it on his own."

"Maybe Chet didn't pay for it," Rose suggested. "Maybe the farmer came back and took the pumpkin away because he didn't get his money."

"If Chet said he paid for it, I doubt he would be lying," Bess sighed. She tapped the top of the table with her fingers. "You know, I still find it odd that one very heavy pumpkin could go missing. I doubt one person would be strong enough to take it, which leads me to wonder about two or more people. What two residents would go to all the trouble of doing that? Is it possible that someone would want to win the Pumpkin Parade that badly?"

No words followed her question. This time, she simply let the topic drift into the air at the center of their table. Bess was slowly coming to the conclusion that this mystery was going to prove difficult to solve with logic and reason.

On her walk home, Bess looked around at the houses she passed. After living on Dogwood Lane for just over a year, she was well acquainted with her neighbors, and she knew which of them were more outgoing. She also began to think about which neighbors had a competitive streak. Yet, despite her familiarity with them, Bess still could not think of a neighbor who was so competitive that they'd roll a hundred pound pumpkin down the street. In fact, no one she knew in her neighborhood, or in the main building, for that matter, had the muscle to remove such a hefty pumpkin.

"There had to be more than one of them," Bess concluded to herself. "One person couldn't have done this. I'm quite certain of that...but that's all I'm certain of."

She stopped in the street to consider her thoughts on the matter. While it was a sound judgment, it still left her with no answers. This mystery gave her something to think about for the rest of the day.

Chapter 13: FORGIVENESS

When she returned home, Bess broke the news to Chet about the missing pumpkin. He seemed as confused as she was over the whole thing, but it didn't seem to get him down. Instead, he went about his schedule for the day, calling his grandson, working on a crossword puzzle and calling some members of his Investment Club to discuss their next meeting.

For lunch, Bess used the last of the tomatoes from her garden to prepare two BLT sandwiches. The smell of bacon filled the kitchen, enhancing her appetite for her sandwich. Together, she and Chet sat at the kitchen table eating and sharing their theories about the missing pumpkin.

The conjecture, as well as their lunch, was interrupted by a knock on the door. Bess put down her sandwich, walked to the door and opened it. She was surprised to find a police officer standing on her front porch. The officer, a tall lean man with a bald head and narrow lips, was standing with two young men. They looked like teenagers, Bess thought. They didn't look too happy to be with the police officer. The young men were taller than the officer. They both had round stomachs, thick necks, and muscular arms that caused Bess to wonder how much they ate every day.

"Is there a Chet Wooden living here?' the policeman asked.

"I'll get him," Bess answered, quickly moving away from the doorway. She could feel her face growing hot as she waved Chet to the door. He stuffed the last of his sandwich in his mouth before getting up from the kitchen table. Still chewing the last of his lunch, Chet nervously pushed his white hair to the side and cleared his throat when he got to the door.

"I'm Chet Wooden," he said. "Can I help you fellas with something?"

"Sorry to bother you," the officer began. "My name is Sherriff Roy Stoobins. These two boys live a few blocks away. They're high school seniors. They also play football at one of the local schools. Seems that last night they were cruising through here when they spotted your pumpkin. I think they liked it because they took it with them."

"My pumpkin?" Chet asked and his eyes shifted to the boys. "Why?"

"Go ahead, boys!" Sherriff Stoobins snapped. "Speak up! I ain't got all day for this nonsense!"

One of the young men, the tallest of the two, stepped forward.

"We had a big football game...so we put your pumpkin on the other team's field before the kickoff. We wrote a note about how they were just a bunch of clowns and how we were gonna kick their butts when we played. It was real funny seeing your clown pumpkin with that note on it."

"And what about my pumpkin?" Chet asked, looking out to the street. "Do you have it with you?"

"No, sir," the boy mumbled. "I'm afraid the other team didn't find it all that funny. I think they got ticked off about what we wrote and they smashed your pumpkin up real good. We were gonna return it, like I told the sheriff, but then it got all messed up. We're sorry, sir."

"You want me to do something?" the sheriff asked.

Chet didn't say much of anything. He thanked the sheriff, chose not to press charges and closed the door.

His head looked down at his shoes and he tucked his hands into his pants' pockets. Bess rubbed his arm and remained silent. When she looked at him, a small smile began to appear on his face.

"Boys will be boys," Chet grinned.

"You're not upset?" Bess asked.

"Of course I'm mad," Chet nodded. "Pressing charges won't get my pumpkin back. No, Bess, this is one of those situations when it's better to forgive and forget."

Bess didn't say anything, but she could feel her eyebrows push together.

"I played football in high school," Chet began. "Of course, you couldn't tell by looking at me now. I was a quarterback back in those days. We had a cross-town rival that we'd play each year. On one occasion, some fellas on the team got me to join them in breaking into the other school to take their mascot, a bulldog named Bruno. Now, in hindsight, it wasn't the smartest thing we did. A janitor caught us and we thought our goose was cooked. He could have called the police, but he didn't. Instead, he gave us a stern talking to, told us he'd call our parents if we tried it again, and sent us on our way."

"Well, that was very nice of him," Bess nodded.

"I've often thought about that moment," Chet nodded. "How different would my life have been if I'd been arrested that night? If I'd gotten mixed up with the wrong crowd? Would I had still been a lawyer? Because one person had it in his heart to forgive my mistake, it made my life better. I wish I would have thanked that man, knowing how my life turned out. That's the power of forgiveness, Bess."

Bess smiled. In her heart, she thought about how good a man Chet was to let those boys off the hook.

She also thought about Donald, her own guilt and the power of forgiveness.

"It looks like another nice day to decorate a pumpkin," Chet observed. "Let me call my farmer friend and see if he can deliver another pumpkin today. Would you be up for another day of making a pumpkin with me?"

"Of course," Bess countered.

Chet stepped into the kitchen and began to call the farmer. Bess stepped outside. The sky was blue. The sun was warm. Bess hoped that another pumpkin would be available. She looked forward to another afternoon spent outside with Chet, working together and talking about things. She also hoped that they could talk some more about forgiveness.

Chapter 14: SOUP AND SENTIMENT

Later that evening, Chet and Bess sat quietly over a dinner of soup and grilled cheese sandwiches. The cool evening air made soup a more inviting dinner than in the heat of the summer. While they enjoyed bowls of tomato soup, Bess and Chet spoke of the events of the day, the new pumpkin they created and the visit from the sheriff.

"It's been a long time since I saw a police officer so close to me," Bess grinned.

"I bet that brought back memories of your days as a police officer," Chet observed.

"*Surprised* would be a better word to describe my reaction," Bess quickly answered. "You're right, though, it actually brought back some memories."

"Well, those boys looked scared," Chet nodded before chomping into his sandwich.

"I was quite surprised at how lenient you were with them," Bess said before blowing on a spoonful of steaming soup. "It makes me mad when I think about it. The nerve of those boys sneaking up to our house in the dark and taking something that didn't belong to them. I would have pressed charges!"

Bess watched Chet quietly sipping his soup and thinking about her words.

"You might be right," Chet answered. "Yet, on some level, I believe those boys were desperate to do something to get their team pumped up for the game. I think they were desperate to win. Desperation can lead people to make bad choices some times."

"I suppose so," Bess slowly nodded and then she grew silent. She dipped her spoon down in her bowl and wiped the corners of her mouth with her napkin. She stared at the small ripples her spoon made in her soup.

"Is something wrong?" Chet asked, glancing over at her bowl. "Did a fly fall in there?"

"No," Bess replied. She looked at Chet, offered him a quick smile, and then began to eat her soup again. "What you said...about being desperate...it just reminded me of something that happened on my train trip home from California."

She turned her eyes back to the small bowl in front of her, stirred the soup and watched the steam spiral up.

"Of course, I don't want to bore you with more stories about my trip. We can talk about something else if you'd like," Bess sighed.

"No, no," Chet said, breaking some crackers into his soup. "I think we've talked enough about those boys stealing our pumpkin. Please, tell me about this desperate train passenger."

"Well, okay," Bess grinned, "but stop me if I'm boring you. I don't want to be one of those old people who blabbers on about things that are inconsequential."

"How could I be bored? I don't think I've ever been on a train. I find every detail you remember fascinating," Chet confessed and he sat back in his seat, looking up in the air for a few seconds to consider his statement. "You seemed to enjoy the experience. Would you consider doing another train trip?"

"Perhaps," Bess replied, glancing up from her bowl. "You see, Chet, as someone with a first class mind and an eye for people, I'm afraid to say that I found my trip out to California rather...dull."

"Dull?" Chet asked and he put his coffee mug down. "You were traveling across this great country with your daughter and granddaughter. I'm certain you had beautiful scenery along the way. How could you be bored?"

"Yes, the views were breathtaking in the beginning," Bess explained and she paused to slip a spoonful of soup in her mouth. "After a while you get used to seeing it. I enjoyed the chance to chat with Samantha and Nicole. From time to time, I'd even pick up a book and read a chapter or two. Yet, while these were all pleasant diversions for me, I still sought out other ways to occupy my mind. More weighty things to think about than what games Nicole liked to play at recess or what the dining car was serving for dinner."

"So you needed some people to watch," Chet laughed and he pointed across the table at her. "I know you, Bess. If there are interesting people around, your mind is instantly engaged."

"You know me too well, dear," Bess grinned and she took a small bite of her grilled cheese sandwich.

"So you didn't have people to watch on the way to California?" Chet asked.

"Oh, there were people…just not interesting ones," Bess sighed. "I think it was because of where we were sitting. Do you remember that Samantha paid for the tickets? Did I mention that she paid extra to get us into first class?"

"Yes, I think I remember you telling me that," Chet said and he rubbed the white whiskers on his unshaved chin and slowly shook his head. "So how could you find traveling in first class boring? Isn't that where all the rich people sit?"

"Not quite," Bess said and she pushed her bowl of soup to the side to cool. "The trip out to California I spent all of my time in first class. I don't know about rich people but there were plenty of business types traveling with us. On the trip out west, I found myself surrounded by well-dressed men and women who looked like they should have been at work. Nearly everyone in first class was dressed in the same nice clothes, they all looked very young, acted far too serious, and spoke softly into their phones quite a bit. While they had a nice appearance, and were well mannered, I found them to be about as engaging as watching oatmeal cool. Their behaviors were far too controlled and predictable for me."

"So what did you do?" Chet asked.

"I decided to go looking for regular people," Bess replied. "I went off in search of passengers who were less disciplined with their emotions."

"And did you find any?" Chet asked.

"On the train ride home, I did," Bess stated, before dipping her spoon into her soup again. "I started wandering beyond the comfortable confines of first class. My curiosity started to lead me into the coach section of the train. It was there I found some interesting people to watch."

"Coach?" Chet laughed and jokingly added, "How beneath you to bother with the common people sitting in coach, Bess."

"Very funny," Bess replied and she reached across the table and gave Chet's hand a playful squeeze.

"So did you find what you were looking for?" Chet asked. "Were there any interesting observations to be made of the common travelers? Any emotions on display that caught your eye?"

"Being in coach was a very different experience," Bess replied and she shook her head when she recalled the details. "I suppose it was due to the cheaper ticket prices, but there were many more people in those train cars than in first class. Of course, when you have more people buying cheaper tickets, it means the seats are smaller and there are fewer amenities to enjoy. Even the aisles were narrower, which made it a challenge for me to move through the cars. There was also a tremendous amount of passenger activity…lots of voices…lots of movement. All in all, I found the coach sections of the train to be a more interesting place."

"So you went there with the intent of finding some interesting people to watch. Did you have any luck?" Chet asked.

"It took a few trips through, but eventually I did find someone," Bess said and she took another bite of her grilled cheese and finished off her soup.

"Only one passenger?' Chet asked. "What made this passenger stand out from the rest?"

"It was a woman I passed once or twice during my travels through coach," Bess recalled, taking her dirty dishes to the sink. "She was always walking around. When we'd pass, she'd always flash a bright smile at me. Sometimes she'd even offer me a pleasantry. Yet, despite her sunny demeanor, she turned out to be quite a desperate person."

"Why?' Chet asked and he leaned forward in his seat. "Why was she so desperate?"

Bess smiled at his apparent interest. She grabbed some saltine crackers from a box on the table, slipped one into her mouth, and carefully considered what she was about to say. She quietly collected her thoughts, looked over at Chet, and began her story.

Chapter 15: A GOOD STORY OVER SUPPER

"So there I was in this cramped, busy train car. I stood in the main aisle and my mind was firing with thoughts about all the people I saw and the activities they were engaged in. On the left side of the aisle, I watched a mother gently patting the bottom of a baby, as if trying to summon up a burp. To my right, laughter could be heard and I managed to catch a glimpse of two young men exchanging high fives while big grins filled their beet-red faces. A few steps down the aisle, I spied a middle-aged man with his head slumped against a window and his eyes closed."

"Sounds like a busy place," Chet mumbled.

"It was," Bess said, and she stood up and carried her soup bowl and spoon to the sink, rinsed them out, then returned to her seat. "I quite enjoyed the atmosphere, Chet. So there I was, walking down the aisle, taking in all those interesting faces when I suddenly realized my path was blocked."

"What do you mean it was blocked?" Chet asked.

"Up ahead, I spotted a train conductor standing in the aisle talking to a passenger. Now they pack a lot of seats into coach, so the aisle was pretty narrow. The closer I got, the more I realized there was simply no way I could get around him," Bess recalled.

"How did you know he was a conductor?" Chet asked.

"It was a guess at first," Bess replied. "The closer I got to him, the more details emerged. I mean he was dressed in a navy blue suit with decorative gold cuffs.

He looked like a young man, standing in the aisle with perfect posture, addressing an older woman who was seated right along the aisle. I recognized her as the same woman I'd passed more than once in the aisle during my journeys into coach. She always smiled at me when we passed and said "hello" to me. Whatever the conductor was telling her…let's just say, she didn't look too happy. In fact, the expression on her face told me she was scared."

"So why didn't you just excuse yourself and walk around the conductor?" Chet asked.

"Because I saw him doing something that piqued my curiosity," Bess answered.

"And what was he doing?" Chet laughed. "Stealing a pumpkin?"

"Of course not," Bess replied.

"Well then, what was it?' Chet asked.

"You see, the longer I watched them," Bess recalled, "the more apparent it became to me that the conductor was speaking quite sternly to the older woman about something of great importance. At one point, I saw him waving his finger wildly in the air. I also noticed how the woman in question merely sat, looking up, her mouth hanging open. Occasionally, she tried to offer something to the conversation but she was always cut off by the conductor. I also remember how her eyes were magnified by her glasses, which made it easier for me to see how frequently they blinked. Sometimes nervous people may say all the right things, but their eyes give so much away."

"So what happened next?" Chet asked.

"Your ticket! I need your ticket!" I heard the conductor demand in a firm tone.

"I already told you I don't have it with me," the woman replied and she shook her head so much her tight white curly hair shook. "Could you come back later? Give me some time to look through my bags."

"We've been over this before, ma'am. I need to check your ticket and I need to do it now," I remember the conductor answered. He took a deep breath and stared down at that poor woman. "I'm not giving you more time to find it. You either have it...or you're in trouble."

"Well, this was just too interesting to walk away from," Bess recalled, looking at Chet. She shrugged her shoulders. "I simply stood behind the conductor and waited to see what would happen next. It was clear to me that the conductor wasn't going to do her any favors. As the seconds went by, I could see this woman's face growing bright red. She fiddled with her hands with a good amount of nervous energy. I was curious to see what was going to happen next."

"So....then what?" Chet asked.

"You can't throw an old lady off the train," I recall the woman saying and she pointed at the conductor like she was daring him to do it.

"That's true; I certainly wouldn't do that," the conductor answered, still not moving an inch. "I think it only fair to warn you, ma'am, that there is another option. You see, if I believe you are travelling on this train with the intent of not paying for a ticket, I'll have someone stay with you on the train and escort you off when we reach a station. Once there, I will have you detained at the station, contact the police, and let them decide to issue you a fine or to charge you with a minor offense."

Bess shook her head at the memories that still lingered in her head. She surprised herself with how well she could recall the words of the conductor.

"I remember it all too well," Bess said, and she tapped her fingers on the table. "That woman had no reply to this warning. She was silent. Her face was now so flushed, her head looked like a ripe tomato. Her mouth hung open. I watched the woman continue to clutch her bags. Despite the conductor's threats, the expression on the woman's face wasn't so much fear…but desperation. Why a woman of this age needed to sneak on a train without a ticket was a question I found too curious to avoid. So I stepped forward and tapped the conductor on the shoulder."

"You didn't!" Chet laughed. "Bess, you certainly have a way of getting yourself right in the middle of things."

"You know me," Bess grinned.

"Well," Chet began. "What happened next? And don't worry about washing the dishes that are stacked in the sink. They can wait. I want to hear how this story ends."

Bess smiled while she let the memoires of the experience flicker in her mind the way movies show in a theater. She thought about what she wanted to say and then she began.

Chapter 16: REMEMBERING THE DESPERATE PASSENGER

"After having me stand just behind him for a few minutes, the conductor finally noticed me. The second we made eye contact, I realized this was my best chance to help. The best approach was to create the stereotypical old confused person, which often lowers people's defenses. I offered him my best old lady smile and then I said six little words in the sweetest tone of voice I could muster.

'Thank you for finding my sister,' I told him and made a point to keep smiling.

'Your sister?' the conductor asked, and he stepped back and his eyes quickly turned to the nice woman he'd been yelling at and then back to me again.

'Yes,' I quickly said, sensing he was confused. 'She belongs with me in first class. That's why she doesn't have a ticket for coach.'

The expression on the woman's face was a perfect blend of confusion and relief.

'There you are, you poor thing!' I said, carefully choosing words that would lead one to feel sympathy. I stepped around the conductor, took the woman by the hand and gently pulled her out of her seat. 'I was beginning to worry about you. You know you forget to take your medicine...and then you wandered off. Every day you do this...you come right back to this same seat and I don't know why. Okay, dear, back to our room. Thank you again, sir.'

Together we slowly moved down the aisle. I looked over my shoulder to see that the conductor still had not moved from his spot.. Because of my age and my words, I knew I'd bought a few seconds to leave that train car. I could tell the conductor was confused by his silence, which played to my advantage.

'But I've seen her here for days,' he finally called out.

'Dementia!' I called back.

Out of the corner of my eye, I could see the conductor, perfect posture and all, still standing in the same spot. I could tell he was trying to process what was happening. Discretion, I told myself, was of the essence. Instead of rushing to leave the car, and the safe confines of first class, I took slow steps, continuing to hold my 'sister' by the hand while I led her out of coach and into the safety of first class.

'Who are you?' the woman whispered.

'I'm the person who's going to save you,' I replied.

When we stepped into the first class train car, a nice young woman asked for our tickets. She was the last attendant to stand between us getting to safety. I showed my ticket to enter the first class car. When the attendant made eye contact with the woman I was escorting, I used my sweetest voice, my best smile, and my most pleasant demeanor to my advantage.

'Does she have a ticket?' the attendant asked.

'My sister wandered off, I sighed and I took her hand in mine. The attendant looked at me. 'She gets confused when she forgets to take her medicine, you know. Does your grandmother have problems with confusion?'

'No,' the train attendant said without expression.

'Wait and she will,' I smiled. 'Getting old isn't for wimps, my dear.'

Sometimes I find that humor can undercut the tension between people. I was hoping this was one of those times. However, the attendant didn't change expression and I became a bit concerned. After a few seconds, a small smile curled under her cheeks.

'Go ahead, ladies,' she said, gesturing for us to pass into the car.

I quickly led my new friend from coach to first class in a matter of seconds. I could only liken it to leading Alice into Wonderland. The second we stepped into first class, the doors closed behind us and silence filled the air. There were no more sounds of people coughing, babies crying, or laughter. Even the air smelled fresher to me. I took a few steps into the empty train car with its broad clear windows and cushioned blue sofas and soft leather chairs. I turned to check on the woman I'd just rescued. She was still clutching a flowery tapestry bag that she carried with her. I smiled and quite suddenly she pulled her hand away from me in a very abrupt way.

'Let go of me,' she snapped.

'Can we sit down here for a minute?' I asked and I gestured to a couple of empty chairs next to a large window.

'I don't want to sit,' the woman grumbled. 'I'm mad. You think I'm confused? You made me sound like I was crazy back there. How dare you say those things about me!'

'I was trying to save you from that conductor,' I pointed out. I was amazed at her objections and couldn't help but shake my head in disbelief at her comments. She should have been grateful.

'I don't need saving,' she snapped.

'Yes, you do,' I quickly replied. 'I doubt you even have a ticket to be on this train. Why should you care what excuse I used to keep you from being caught? You should be thanking me for getting you out of trouble with that conductor. We both know you don't have a ticket.'

'How do you know I *don't* have a ticket?' the woman quickly asked and she began to dig through her tapestry bag. 'I'll tell you what I told the conductor...I do have a ticket! I must have misplaced it in my bag, that's all.'

I smiled at her persistence so I gave her a minute and encouraged her to dig through her rather large tapestry bag. Watching her dig through the bag, I knew it wouldn't take her all that long to find a ticket...if she had one. After giving her a generous amount of time, I saw her eyes glance at me. That's when I knew she didn't have a ticket. That's when I knew it was time to share my observations.

'You know I've walked through coach a few times during this trip,' I explained. 'I've seen you more than once moving around the train car. What I noticed is that you're always very pleasant when you see me. I can also conclude that you tend to walk in the aisles more than the other passengers. At first I thought it was just for exercise, or maybe curiosity like me, but now I realize there's more to it. I'd be willing to guess you timed your walks around the time when the conductor appeared in your train car to check for tickets.'

'I have a ticket,' the woman stated again and she started to dig through her bag one more time.

'Stop looking in there and look at me,' I finally said.

She turned her face to me and away from her bag.

'If you have a ticket,' I said and I pointed over the woman's shoulder, 'then accept my apology and return to your seat in coach. I'm quite certain the conductor will be waiting for you. If I'm right, then sit down with me and let's get to know each other better.

Much to my surprise, the woman closed her bag. She turned and looked back at the door that led back to coach. I thought she was going to stand up and head for the door. Instead, she looked at me and the bitter expression on her face began to shift and change and turn into a more relaxed look.

'Fine,' the woman muttered and she settled into a chair. 'So here we are. Tell me, why are you're doing this?'

'Let me answer that with another question,' I suggested, sitting down in a chair so we could face each other. 'Tell me why someone would go to the trouble of boarding a train without a ticket? You don't appear to be a thief or a smuggler. I doubt money is the motivator here. The only other reason I can think of for you to sneak on this train is desperation.'

I paused for a moment for her to reply, but she remained silent and simply stared at me.

'You see,' I continued, 'it would take someone very desperate to go to the trouble of slipping onto a train and risk being caught. I mean those penalties that the conductor was talking about sounded pretty severe to me. You must have known what the risks were when you decided to do it.'

The woman didn't answer. I watched her eyes turn away from me to the pleasant scenery outside the window. I couldn't tell if she was listening to me or simply lost in her thoughts.

'The trick is to move around when they come to check for tickets,' the woman explained with a sense of pride in her voice. 'Just be very subtle and move to open seats when you can. I could always see when the conductor was entering the train car. That's when I'd simply go to the bathroom, come out and find a seat to talk with someone in another section that was already checked. I was quite good at keeping my eye on that conductor and being very discreet at moving around the train car. You saw how many passengers are back there. It wasn't too hard for me to get lost in the shuffle.'

'It sounds like a good system,' I said. 'So how did you finally get caught?'

'I made the mistake of falling asleep,' the woman replied. 'You know that tapping sound the train makes against the rails? I find it quite soothing when I close my eyes. Unfortunately, I drifted off back there and when I woke up, I found the conductor standing right beside me asking for my ticket.'

'And so this brings me back to my original question,' I began. I paused and looked around to see if anyone was close to us. I leaned in and used the softest voice I could for my next question. 'Why are you taking such a risk?'

The woman leaned forward in her seat and pointed at me.

'Are you a mother?' the woman whispered.

'Yes,' I answered.

'Then you know the one thing that would cause a mother to take such a chance,' the woman explained. 'What does a mother care about more than anything? Who would a mother risk everything for?'

'Their child,' I nodded.

'I have a daughter who is about to have an operation,' the woman explained. 'She said she'll be fine, but she has three young children to care for. She is a single mother, which is hard work. Once her surgery is complete, she'll be in bed for a few weeks after the surgery. I'm the only family she has.'

When she finished speaking, I watched her sit back in her seat. With her glasses magnifying her eyes, it was easy for me to see her blink a few times, like she was processing what she'd just told me.

'I'm not the richest person in the world,' she finally spoke, and she looked right at me. 'Far from it. In fact, I've long since retired from work and I have little of any retirement savings to live on. However, my daughter is my world. I want to be there for her. That's why I'm on this train without a ticket. I have to get to Pennsylvania. I have to be there for my daughter. If I can stay on this train until tomorrow, then I'll be able to help her.'"

Chapter 17: RECOLLECTION RESOLVED

When Bess finished her story, she helped Chet clear the dinner table and wash the dishes in the sink. While they worked, they commented on the quality of the tomato soup and debated the merits of having it again. Once all the dishes were put away, Chet suggested they step out on the back porch to enjoy the sunset.

The evening sky held a blue hue that gave way to more vivid colors of pink, gold and red following the setting sun. Bess and Chet settled into their favorite deck chairs and watched the sky grow flush as the sun began to melt into the horizon like a small scoop of butter.

"So what did you do about her?" Chet asked, looking up at the sky.

"Who?" Bess asked.

"The woman on the train," Chet replied. "The one without the ticket."

"I helped her, of course," Bess replied.

"You helped someone break a rule?" Chet asked, and his eyes turned away from the colors above to look at Bess. "You never cease to surprise me, sweetheart."

"So I helped a desperate mother for one night," Bess answered and she shook her head. "The world wasn't going to end. Besides, it gave me time to think of something other than grieving for Donald."

"So how did you conceal her?" Chet asked. "Did you have any excitement keeping other people from being suspicious of her?"

"I'm afraid there really was no added excitement," Bess answered. "I let her stay in first class. We were only one day out from our return. That evening she ate with Samantha, Nicole, and me in the dining car. She was a very friendly woman to talk to. Later that night, when we went to our sleeping cabin, that woman simply dozed off in a chair in one of the observation cars."

"Didn't anyone notice her?" Chet asked.

"Most of those young business travelers had their noses in their phones," Bess recalled. "In the morning, I found her with a blanket over her waist. I let her in our sleeping cabin to freshen up and then she joined us for breakfast. While eating waffles, I found out her name was Pauline. At least, that's what she told us. Then, when we arrived at the station, Pauline simply slipped away with the other passengers and that was that."

"Not even a "thank-you?" Chet asked.

"Not that I recall," Bess mumbled.

"How rude," Chet mumbled.

"Too desperate for manners, I'd suppose," Bess sighed.

"You really took a risk helping her," Chet said. "In the end, was it really worth all that trouble?"

"It's not like I made a conscious choice to find someone to help," Bess sighed, turning away from the lush tones of the sky to look at Chet. "I was led by instinct. It was instinct that drew me into the situation. It was the expression I saw on her face when being confronted by the conductor. It was the tone in her voice when she spoke back to him. It was the way she clutched her bags with such fear; I could see her knuckles were clearly white. I've been around long enough to know the difference between someone who is clever versus someone who is honest. Those were my reasons why I was drawn in."

"And Samantha didn't mind?' Chet asked. "You know she's always a stickler about following the rules."

"Having a guest at our dinner table, and concealing it…that was tricky," Bess recalled. "Things went much smoother the next morning. It seemed that the closer we got to Pennsylvania, the more Samantha's phone took her focus away from our guest. I swear, Chet, I could have jumped off that train and my daughter wouldn't have noticed…unless I called her on her phone to tell her."

They both laughed at the observation. Silence filled the evening air. The light around them was beginning to fade. Fireflies were now swirling in their backyard. The sky was a brilliant shade of violet with a ribbon of golden light shooting out from the horizon.

"When I think about it," Bess finally began. "It was one example of how riding on a train simply leads complete strangers to bond with each other. Of course, there were people who hopped on at some stations and got off at others, but there was a small group of us who were going from one coast to the other. They were passengers with whom I shared this experience."

"I'd imagine you do form a bond with other people in that situation," Chet stated.

"It's inevitable," Bess nodded. "At first, we'd smile politely at each other when we'd pass. Then we started to make conversation about the scenery or the experiences of being on the train. Sometimes we'd see each other in the dining cars and comment on the quality of the superb meals they served us. Soon, I began to realize I knew all of these friendly faces…but I didn't know any names. I'd suppose that's how it is when you travel with a large group like I did."

"Well, that one stranger was very lucky that you found her," Chet said.

"Yes," Bess agreed. "Whether riding a train car without a ticket, or stealing a large pumpkin, desperate people make for the most interesting stories."

Together they sat and watched the clouds turn from golden to the kind of blue one would associate with pen ink. The sky surrendered to a very dark shade of purple. A few birds chirped from the trees. The fireflies filled the yard with magic.

Chapter 18: A CURIOUS MARK

As the days went by, it became apparent to Bess that autumn had settled in and was now in full swing at the Honey Hills Retirement Community. The warm days were growing cooler. The colorful leaves that had once filled the trees were turning dry and brown and tumbling in the wind. For Bess, it was close to the time when she would bid a reluctant farewell to her garden before a long winter break.

Her husband, Chet, was caught up in the autumn spirit. With his back still on the mend, he drove to a variety of farm markets and grocery stores in search of the perfect apple cider. Chet thoroughly enjoyed apple cider and drank it every morning with his nose in the business section of the newspaper. Occasionally, in the afternoons, she also spotted him with a glass of apple cider while he worked on a crossword puzzle. This afternoon, he was outside raking some leaves while talking about how he would reward himself with a glass of apple cider when he was finished. While she knew Chet missed attending Waltzing Club meetings, she hoped that there was something in apple cider that was making his back feel good enough to do some raking.

With the sound of Chet's raking in the air, Bess knelt down by her gardens and took one last look at what scraps of life remained. She removed the brown stems and withered flowers and began to make a neat pile beside her gardens. The sight of Chet being outside with her, doing yard work, simply made her smile. It was good to see him outside instead of sitting at the kitchen table reading a newspaper or doing a crossword puzzle.

While they worked together in the yard, Bess glanced over to her neighbor's yard and felt her curiosity rise. What she saw caused her to stand up, drop some weeds on the ground and carefully step out of her garden.

Moving through her backyard, Bess quietly walked into her neighbor's yard. She stopped in front of a wash line that had been tied between a tree and a pole. Her eyes lingered on the assortment of clothes that were hanging from the line. Shirts, pants, and skirts fluttered in the afternoon breeze. What drew her attention was a particularly small piece of clothing that dangled from the line.

It was an article of clothing that any mother would recognize. Clothing that tugged at her maternal instincts. Bess stepped closer, reached out, and gently brushed her hand across a small pink body suit that appeared to belong to a very young child. She let her fingers linger on the baby outfit. She tugged at the little feet at the bottom of the garment and she could feel her lips turn up at the corners. She leaned in, sniffed the outfit and felt the sweet smells of a baby fill her heart.

"Good morning, Bess," a voice called out.

Bess quickly let go of the baby suit when she saw her neighbor, Connie Ocker, step out of her house and walk through her backyard to where Bess was standing. Bess pointed at the outfit and smiled.

"This is an unusual thing to find with your wash," Bess smiled. "I'm used to seeing slacks, shirts, and the occasional undergarments flapping from your wash line. Not that I'm nosey, Connie, it's just that when I'm working in my garden or sitting on my back porch, the clothes on your wash line are hard to ignore. This baby outfit is adorable. Who does it belong to?"

"That outfit belongs to my granddaughter. She stays with us on Tuesdays," Connie explained. "She's only a year old. My daughter and her husband are both back at work. They have a one hour window when she goes to work and he comes home that they have me watch my sweet granddaughter. It's the best part of my week."

"When my granddaughter comes it makes me smile," Bess replied.

"Have you and Chet enjoyed the pumpkin pie?" Connie asked.

"It tastes very good," Bess nodded.

"Well, it's a little something to help with the grief," Connie smiled.

Bess smiled and glanced back at the baby outfit one more time When she moved her eyes from the baby outfit to focus on Connie, Bess noticed that Connie was rubbing one hand with the other. It was warm in the sunshine, so Bess wasn't sure if Connie was cold or if something else was bothering her hand.

"Connie, are you a little chilly?" Bess asked.

"No," Connie answered.

"The way you're rubbing your hands together on this mild day," Bess observed, "it just seems to me that you might need to slip a jacket on."

"It's actually just the one hand I'm rubbing," Connie explained. "One hand that's not cold…just sore."

Bess looked down and was shocked when Connie revealed the hand she was rubbing. What Bess saw was a large oval-shaped bruise on the back of Connie's hand. The oval was maroon, with two purple dots at the center of the circle.

"My goodness, that looks sore," Bess said and she tipped her head to one side and pointed at the wound. "What on earth happened to you, Connie? Did you have an accident?"

"There was this therapy dog," Connie began. "His name is Buster. He comes to the main building to visit every Tuesday and Thursday. I've seen the dog and spoke to his owner, Marty Clark, a few times. She's very nice. So this morning I saw Marty and Buster walking towards the main building from the parking lot. Buster must have been excited to get inside because he was pulling hard on his leash. Of course, I smiled and waved to Marty and we started to talk. Buster was still pulling on his leash and I went to pet him to calm him down. I've pet Buster many times, but on this particular morning when I reached for him he jumped up and nipped me on the hand."

"You poor thing," Bess replied, shaking her head. "Well, that looks like more than a nip to me, Connie. He really sank his teeth into you. Did you have a nurse look at it?"

"Marty said the dog has all of its shots," Connie replied. "She really was quite embarrassed and apologized a lot. I don't want to get Marty in trouble, so I didn't say anything to the nurses. She is so loyal about bringing Buster here every Tuesday for residents to meet and pet. He's usually such a good dog. I'll just have to be a little more careful in how I approach Buster when I go to pet him. He's visiting the main building, so I hope he doesn't bite anyone else."

"But Connie," Bess said. "Buster is a therapy dog. He shouldn't be biting anyone if he's coming here."

"Animals aren't always predictable, Bess," Connie warned. "I grew up on a farm. When you're around animals...you learn that they can be moody...just like people."

Bess smiled at Connie's words. However, she still felt a sense of urgency about the matter. If the dog was sick, or simply in a bad mood as Connie had suggested, someone should warn the residents in the main building. Without saying another word, Bess set off to see if she could find Marty and Buster.

Chapter 19: BUSTER

Ever since she lived in the main building, Bess had grown accustomed to seeing Marty and Buster pass through the building. On a typical visit, they would come late in the morning and walk through the halls greeting any resident who stopped to meet Buster. Marty was a very social person and always enjoyed talking to any resident who stopped. Buster was an old Cocker Spaniel who enjoyed belly rubs and sniffing the hand of any resident who'd pet him. Bess could easily recall seeing Marty in a sitting room, chatting with residents for hours while Buster sat on the floor next to her chair. Knowing how much Marty loved to chat, Bess was hoping to find her in the main building socializing.

When she reached the entrance to the main building, Bess spotted a woman sitting on the bench by the main doors. She was wearing a lavender dress with white shoes that matched her hair. The woman smiled at Bess.

"Hello," the woman said, adjusting her tight white curls.

"Hello," Bess replied. "Lovely day to be out."

"Yes, it is," the woman grinned.

As Bess entered the building, she thought about the simple pleasure that came from exchanging kind words with another resident. She was quite proud to be part of a generation that complimented each other with a smile or a spoken word and not just a short text message. She didn't need a cell phone or a computer to be kind. On occasion, it was simply nice to watch a person react to a compliment.

Once inside the building, Bess began to roam the hallways, hoping that she'd catch a glimpse of Buster or Marty. Of course, in coming so often for visits, Buster was very well known by both residents and nurses. With that in mind, Bess stepped over to the closest nurse's station to ask for some help in finding Buster.

"Excuse me," she began. "Have you seen Buster here today? He's a therapy dog."

"Yes, I know who Buster is," the nurse replied and she smiled. "I just saw him a little while ago. He must be around here somewhere."

Suddenly one distinct bark filled the air. The nurse's head snapped in the direction of the bark and she began to laugh.

"There's your answer," the nurse grinned and she pointed down one hallway in the direction of the bark.

Bess immediately set off. She quickly moved down one corridor, turned a corner, and then strolled into a sitting area where she heard another bark. Bess spotted Marty open a door to the Dementia Unit and slip inside. Bess picked up her pace and quickly followed through the doors. Once in the Dementia Unit, she found Buster pulling Marty down the hall. The small golden Cocker Spaniel yanked hard on his leash while Marty spoke firmly to him. She then stopped in the hallway and stepped in front of Buster, who still didn't seem to be paying much attention to her commands.

"Sit! I said sit!" Marty ordered in a firm voice.

Buster seemed to ignore her command, sniffing the floor with wild abandon, pulling hard on his leash again to follow his nose.

"Hello, Marty," Bess smiled. She had met Marty before and had always enjoyed petting Buster when he visited. "How's my favorite dog doing today?"

"I'm afraid he's not being a very good listener," Marty replied and she frowned down at the bundle of golden fur and energy at the end of the leash.

"He looks...frisky," Bess observed. "I know he's old...but it's nice to see that he still has a little puppy in him."

She watched the buff-colored Cocker Spaniel snatch his leash in his mouth and begin to shake his head from side to side with such vigor that his whiskers fluffed out. Marty reached down, jerked the leash from his mouth and waved her finger at him the way a mother would discipline a child.

Bess smiled at two ladies who were sitting on a couch laughing at Buster's frisky demeanor. As she watched Marty tangle with Buster, something revealed itself to Bess. While everyone was so focused on the behavior of the dog, which was adorable, no one was watching the expression on the face of the owner. It was that expression, which caused Bess to look a little harder at Marty.

The tone in Marty's voice, the look in her eyes, and the expression on her face told Bess that Marty was not in control of Buster. This wasn't the same Marty doing yet another typical visit to the retirement home. Rather than being in control of the situation, Marty appeared to be surprised by Buster's behavior. As a therapy dog, it was clear to Bess that Buster should be anything but unpredictable.

"Is Buster feeling okay?" Bess finally asked.

"He's...fine," Marty answered, and she reached down and brushed her fingers through his caramel-colored fur. Buster finally sat down. "He just has a little spring in his step today."

"I ran into Connie Ocker this morning," Bess continued. "She has a nasty mark on her hand from Buster. Did he bite her?"

"Unfortunately, he did," Marty stated. She looked at Bess and her eyes grew wide from behind her glasses. "Please don't tell anyone. I feel so badly about it."

"I won't tell," Bess answered and she looked around at some of the dementia residents walking around smiling at Buster. "Marty, I don't think it's safe to have Buster here. If he bit Connie, he might do it again. Is he acting this way because he's sick?"

"He's not sick," Marty answered, and she stopped petting Buster. Marty kept looking at her dog and offered no other words to describe the dog's behavior, which Bess found rather odd.

"I've seen you bring Buster in here many times, Marty," Bess continued. "He's always been such a sweet dog. You and I have spoken at lengths about how calm a dog he is and how good he is for residents to see. In all of your visits, I've never seen him pull on his leash or ignore your commands in the retirement home. I've never heard him bark."

Marty kept her eyes locked on Buster and remained silent. She reached down and nervously stroked the side of the dog's stomach with her hand.

"Marty?' Bess asked and she looked down at the dog and back at Marty. "I'm not going to be the only resident who sees these differences. I suspect that's why you came to the Dementia Unit today. Residents here aren't so good with…details."

Silence filled the air. Marty continued to pet Buster, who was now stretched out on the floor fast asleep.

"You know," Marty began, "it is such a joy to come here. Such a joy to watch residents light up when they see my little dog in the hallway. So many residents just want to have an animal to pet, or talk to, or love. It would be a shame for everyone if I couldn't come around here any more."

Marty looked up at Bess and her face looked a little sad. Her mouth dipped at the corners and the creases on her face shifted to give her a more sullen expression.

"What's the matter, Marty?" Bess asked.

"I'm afraid," Marty mumbled.

"Afraid of what?" Bess asked.

"Afraid of someone noticing changes in Buster," Marty replied.

Bess looked down at the dog quietly resting on the floor. She looked back at Marty and was surprised to see her reach up with her hand and wipe a tear from her cheek. Bess could sense that a swell of emotion had come over Marty but she wasn't sure why.

"Marty?" Bess said softly. She moved and sat down beside Marty. "Marty? Are you okay? Did I say something to upset you?"

"No," Marty answered with a soft, wispy voice. "It's just that...."

"What?' Bess pressed.

Marty looked down at the dog curled up by her feet. She sniffed and reached down to pet him one more time.

"Buster is dead," Marty finally said.

Chapter 20: THE DEAD DOG

"Dead?" Bess asked, stunned by the news and her eyes quickly went down to look at the dog curled up at Marty's feet. She scanned every inch of the dog and then pointed at it. "Marty, are you telling me this isn't Buster? It certainly looks like him."

"You see, Buster died a few weeks ago," Marty began. "I left the gate open in the backyard when I was pruning some shrubs. I completely forgot that Buster was in the yard with me. Before I knew it, he'd wandered out through the gate. Then I heard a car horn and before I knew it Buster was hit. The loss has been just devastating for me. Have you every noticed how that is, Bess? When it takes a long time for death to run its course, somehow the grief just isn't that strong. It's when the death comes swiftly, like it did for poor Buster, that it makes grief so much harder to handle."

"Grief and guilt," Bess replied, her brother's face flashing in her mind. "My husband died of cancer and he suffered for a long time. It was a relief when he passed. My brother died quite unexpectedly a few weeks ago. I'm still trying to come to grips with it."

Bess was surprised at how much she had just shared in one breath. It seemed like something inside of her simply couldn't wait for the words to fly out.

"So there I was," Marty continued, "sitting in my house for about a week, staring at Buster's dog dish and my heart just ached for him. The house was too quiet and too empty. That's when I knew what I had to do."

"And what was that?" Bess asked.

"I started driving to various animal shelters looking for another cocker spaniel," Marty replied. "It just so happened that in one particular shelter I saw a dog, this dog, which bore a striking resemblance to Buster. Same caramel color. Same rounded snout. Same nub of a tail. It just made me feel good taking him home."

"They could be twins," Bess agreed.

"Now this new Buster is a few years younger than the one that died," Marty explained. "That's why he's not as well behaved, but I'm training him. While I suspect a few people might notice the difference, I also know the residents here at the Honey Hills Center are counting on seeing a dog. I'm training him as best I can, but right now I'm only taking him to the Dementia Unit. I ran into Connie at the entrance. That was an accident. I don't plan on stopping for anyone else except the dementia patients."

"My dear," Bess began and she pointed down at the dog. "While your dedication for visiting the residents here is from the heart, I think it's important for your new dog to complete its training first. Have you signed him up for any obedience classes? Any training classes so he can be a therapy dog like the other Buster?"

"We start next week," Marty answered. "Like I said, I've been working with him at home. Therapy training will take a few weeks. My instinct told me to get him in here first to see the other residents. I thought getting people around him, letting him get used to them, would be a good idea. It was just unfortunate that he bit Connie."

"The Honey Hills Center isn't going anywhere," Bess stated. "Take your dog and get him trained, Marty. Bring him back in a few weeks. It'll be more enjoyable for you and for us to know he's not going to nip at any more residents."

Marty smiled. The new Buster sat up, turned his head to the side and laid his dark brown eyes on Bess. It seemed to Bess that Buster had a sixth sense for knowing when someone was talking about him.

"Thank you for your concern," Marty said, and she tugged on Buster's leash. "I think I know what's best for my dog."

She then turned and headed back down the hallway, smiling to more dementia patients along the way. Bess watched Marty stop to let another resident comment on the dog. She lingered in the hallway, watching the resident reach down and smile while the new Buster jumped around with boundless energy.

Bess hoped that the new Buster didn't get Marty in trouble. It was one of those situations, Bess told herself, where she couldn't force someone to make the right choice. Marty was a grown woman with a sense of purpose in bringing Buster around. Bess only hoped that the new Buster didn't get into any more trouble with his frisky nature and his sharp teeth.

Chapter 21: THE LINGERING FOG

While she took the memories of frisky Buster to bed with her, and chuckled with Chet over the dog's behavior, darker feelings crept into her thoughts when she closed her eyes. She could feel the guilt of her brother coming back to her in the form of a dream. The feelings filled her heart and threaded their way into her memories, pulling forth images of her trip. When Bess woke up, she pushed the sheets off her legs and sat up in her bed.

"Chet," Bess whispered, and she reached over and shook her husband awake.

"What's wrong?" Chet mumbled and he sat up. "Are you okay?"

"I was dreaming about the funeral," Bess sighed and she sat up in bed.

"I'm sorry," Chet sighed, and he reached over and gently wrapped his large hand over her smaller one. "It was a terrible day…but you just had a bad dream, Bess. Hold my hand and try to go back to sleep."

As was sometimes the case after a bad dream, she was afraid to close her eyes again. She was afraid that the same dream would pick right up with her. She rubbed her eyes and tried to fight the urge to go back to sleep.

"After the funeral, Chet, I took a walk by myself," Bess began, uncertain of how carefully Chet was listening to her.

"Where did you go?" Chet's gravelly voice spoke from the darkness.

"Donald had this beautiful home right by the ocean," Bess recalled. "That's where we gathered after the funeral with his family. Donald's widow, his children, the grandchildren, Samantha, Nicole and myself. That morning, when we got back from the cemetery, I just couldn't listen to all the voices in that house. I heard voices telling stories, some voices laughing, and I just needed a moment to myself. So I stepped outside, lingered on his back porch and then stepped right onto the beach."

Bess lay back down and stared into the darkness over her bed.

"I stood on the beach, Chet, and closed my eyes and felt the sun in my face," Bess continued. "I stood there with my eyes shut and listened to the sea crash and sizzle on the sand. I could smell the ocean air. It was all salty and fresh and it rolled over my face like a wave on the sand and I thought of Donald."

"That sounds nice," Chet whispered.

"When I opened my eyes, I looked out as far as I could," Bess continued. "My eyes went out to where the sky met the sea. That's when I thought about Donald. How many times did he step off his porch and stand on that very same spot? How many times did he look at the water or the sky and voice his hopes, his wishes, and his concerns. I stood there wishing that the sky and the sea could speak to me. I wished they could tell me all the thoughts and wishes my brother made over the years. Looking at that view was like being in the company of a quiet friend of my brother...a quiet friend who was good at keeping my brother's secrets. I just wish I knew what he thought in his last days."

"You called him a few times a week when he was being treated," Chet recalled.

"I know we talked about his treatments," Bess recalled. "Our conversations were always at the surface.

Donald never liked to have deep conversations. I often wondered what he thought about what was happening to him."

"Some secrets we just keep to ourselves, Bess," Chet yawned.

"I suppose you're right," Bess replied and she shifted her head on her pillow. "You know, Chet, his wife told me that her grief was like a fog that had settled over her life. You know when you're driving somewhere and you drive through a patch of fog? You know how you can't see anything off either side of the road, but you just keep driving and hope you eventually get out of the fog? That's how I've been feeling, Chet. I feel like I'm never going to find the end to this fog, but I keep going every day. I keep busy. I keep looking for mysteries to solve. I keep going to bridge club. I keep thinking that tomorrow will be the day that the fog will clear."

"One day it will," Chet sighed.

She leaned close, kissed Chet on the cheek, and then turned on her side. When she closed her eyes, she drifted back to sleep thinking of the day when her guilt and her mourning would subside.

Chapter 22: LOVE AND ELECTIONS

The next morning, Bess was able to focus on something other than her grief. It was Election Day. While it wasn't time to elect a new president, there were still many state and local offices that were up for grabs. The Honey Hills Retirement Center was a designated voting location for people in the township to come and cast their vote. As a result, Bess saw more traffic on Dogwood Lane then she'd ever seen before. The quiet confines of living on the grounds of a retirement home were lost to younger people. They were easy to spot, quickly driving down her street at a speed far greater than the posted fifteen-mile-per-hour limit.

In all of her years, Bess had never missed casting her vote on Election Day. This morning would be no exception. She got up early to cast her vote. She dressed, then stepped into the kitchen where she was surprised to find Chet unshaven, still in his pajamas, sipping coffee while reading the newspaper.

"Chet?" Bess asked, a bit confused by the scene. "Aren't you coming? It's Election Day so we have to go vote."

"Not me," Chet grunted while he read his paper. "I don't need to change my morning routine for crooks and thieves."

"Well," Bess sighed, "I haven't missed a vote in my life and I'm not about to start skipping elections this morning. I understand they're serving coffee and doughnuts at the voting center. I'll bring a doughnut back for you, dear."

"That's okay," Chet said, waving one hand in the air. "I just finished breakfast. Go ahead and vote."

It was a rare occasion for Bess to leave the house without breakfast but such was the case this morning. She grabbed a thick coat, given the early morning hour, and stepped outside. She shivered at the crisp autumn air and thought briefly about asking Chet to drive her there. Then she thought about that warm cup of coffee waiting for her at the voting center and picked up the pace heading down Dogwood Lane.

The sky was overcast and the clouds resembled a sheer white scarf being pulled in front of the sun, making it look more like a round pearl. Walking down her street, she began to see small cardboard signs attached to wooden stakes. When she got closer to one of the sign, she noticed the words, *This Way to Vote* above an arrow pointing the way. She turned at one sign and followed a sidewalk to another sign, which directed her to make a right turn.

"This is like a scavenger hunt," Bess mumbled to herself.

Eventually she found herself heading towards the main building of the Honey Hills Center. Yet another sign pointed her to a rear access door located next to a gift shop. Bess walked through that door and immediately heard voices in an auditorium. When she arrived, she was surprised to find a long line of residents waiting for their turn in one of five voting booths. Bess quickly estimated about fifty people in the line. She drew in her breath, undid her coat, and resigned herself to a long wait.

"Where's the coffee?" Bess whispered to herself, and her eyes began to scan the room for what she desired most. "Goodness, I hope they have coffee."

"Hello, Bess," a perky voice spoke.

She looked around to find Alma Crisp standing towards the front of the line, well ahead of Bess. Alma waved for Bess to come up and join her. At first, Bess shook her head, mindful of the other people ahead of her. Alma continued to gesture until Bess finally stepped by ten other residents to stand with her friend. Bess was quite mindful of the grumbling words she heard as she stepped up to the front of the line.

"It's okay," Alma called back to the unhappy faces in line. "She has to take some medicine any time now. She really needs to be up here with me."

"I have to take medicine, too! You don't see me cutting to the front of the line!" a woman's voice barked from the middle of the room.

Alma simply smiled and waved at the faces behind her, then turned to Bess and grinned like a school girl who'd just broken a class rule.

"Really, Alma," Bess whispered. "That really wasn't necessary."

"Sorry," Alma beamed. "It's just such a long wait in line and...well...I have someone that I'd like you to meet."

Alma grabbed the arm of a man in a brown tweed jacket standing in front of her. He slowly turned, and the first thing Bess noticed were his side burns, which were white and bushy. While the top of his head didn't have much hair, he more than made up for it with the two puffy side burns that looked like caterpillars climbing along his cheeks. He offered Bess a smile and she could see through his glasses how his eyes squinted together when he grinned.

"Bess," Alma said. "This is Paul Ford. This is the man I told you about. Paul, this is one of the ladies from my bridge club. The one I write about on my blog."

"The detective?" Paul asked. "I've read all of Alma's blogs. What you do is very interesting, Mrs. Bullock."

"You can call me Bess," she smiled.

Paul stepped back and looked Bess up and down.

"My, aren't you a little thing?" Paul observed. "You must have been one tough police officer. Were you always this small or is it just old age?"

"I was never that big," Bess confessed.

"I can't imagine how you handled the bad guys back then," Paul grinned.

"Mind over muscle was my motto," Bess replied.

"And today?" Paul inquired.

"There aren't a whole lot of bad guys living here at the Honey Hills Center," Bess stated, "unless, of course, you count those people standing in line behind us. I don't think they're too happy with me right now."

"The only unhappy people here are the ones who look for things to be unhappy about," Alma quickly surmised. "I think those people complaining behind us were unhappy long before you arrived, Bess. They were unhappy about the wait. Then they were unhappy about their choices for voting. I could hear them back there. Don't feel bad."

"My sweet Alma," Paul gushed and he leaned over and kissed her on the cheek. "That's what I love about you. Not many people can take a problem and spin it that way. That's why you're my glass-half-full girl."

"She is that," Bess said and she offered a nod. "Alma has always been able to find the good in situations. As Alma might have told you, I was out of town for a few weeks. It's nice to finally meet you, Mr. Ford."

"Paul," he answered and he offered a red-faced smile after the comment. "Any friend of Alma's is a friend of mine. So please call me Paul."

"Okay, Paul," Bess smiled. "So Alma hasn't told me too much about you, other than that she loves you."

Alma giggled and dipped her head down.

"Well, I was born and raised in Pittsburgh, Pennsylvania," Paul began. "After college, I got a job with Petroleum Steel. I took a position with the company and managed a steel foundry on the outskirts of Pittsburgh, which is where I raised my family. My wife died about ten years ago. I never thought I'd find love again…. then I met Alma."

"You know, Paul," Alma spoke, "Bess met someone here at Honey Hills, just like us. They were married shortly after they met."

"Well, that is fine to hear," Paul said, turning to Bess. "So you know the joy that Alma and I have been experiencing. Falling in love this late in life is such a pleasant surprise."

"I told Bess about our plans for marriage," Alma spoke.

"Actually, Alma, those are your plans," Paul said. "Right now, I just love being with you. I love every hour I'm with my sweet Alma. Marriage will come later."

"I see," Bess nodded.

"Alma told me you were married here at Honey Hills. Where is your husband?" Paul asked.

"At home," Bess answered and she rolled her eyes after she spoke. "He tells me that he doesn't vote for crooks. I think he's just grumpy because of his sore back. I'm afraid he feels that honesty is in short supply when it comes to politicians. What are your thoughts on honesty, Paul? Are you like my husband? Do you feel it's in short supply too?"

"I'm afraid it might be in politics," Paul said. He gestured with his hands at the people in line. "I think it's up to the common people to keep them honest.

That's why good honest people like us have to vote. That's why I didn't mind the foul words coming from the back of the line. Those folks were just being honest about how they felt about you cutting in line. Nothing wrong with honesty. I bet they're still pretty steamed with you."

Bess could feel her face grow flush and she tried not to think about the angry residents fuming behind her. Still part of her was tempted to look over her shoulder to catch a glimpse of the expressions on their faces.

"So where did you two meet?" Bess finally asked, trying to get her mind focused on something different.

"We met at a lecture on Winston Churchill," Alma replied. "You see, Churchill's granddaughter wrote a book about her memories of him. Paul and I bumped into each other at a coffee social after the lecture. You know, Paul served in the army. So we had a wonderful conversation about his service and then we said goodbye. The very next day we bumped into each other again. This time we were sharing a table for Bingo. We talked so much that we got shushed by a couple of ladies at the table beside ours. They told us to leave if we were going to talk. So we did. We took a walk outside and admired the leaves. By the end of the walk, I think I knew."

"So did I," Paul grinned.

"Knew what?" Bess asked, a bit confused.

"You know," Alma grinned and she gestured to her and Paul.

"Oh," Bess laughed, and she waved her hand and felt her face grow warm.

For the next few minutes, the conversation fluttered around a wide range of topics. Occasionally, the line moved. Alma and Paul used the situation to give Bess more details about their relationship, their mutual love of *Perry Mason* and details about their dates. Bess simply smiled and nodded politely. Without much prompting, Alma and Paul continued to fill in the blanks on the beginnings of their courtship.

While they spoke to her, Bess became less focused on judging their words as a measure of their love. She smiled and nodded to everything they said, but she was more focused on the details that her eyes picked up on. She noticed the occasional way Paul gently placed his hand on the back of Alma's waist, guiding her forward before him when the line moved. She saw how the back of their hands would brush against each other when they were down by their sides, and their fingers would lace together. She noticed how one of them would occasionally finish the other's sentence. Taken as a whole, their words and gestures told Bess everything she needed to know about what was in their hearts.

Soon it was Bess's turn to place her vote. After making her selections, Bess made her way over to a table where coffee was being served. She grabbed a cup, took a deep sip and let the flavors wake up her senses. When she reached for a doughnut, she was surprised at what was on the table.

"Pumpkin pie?" Bess asked.

She shot a disapproving glance at the volunteer standing at the table.

"Help yourself," the woman grinned.

"I don't really have pie for breakfast," Bess explained. "I told my husband I'd bring a doughnut with me when I came home. Where are they?"

"Well," the volunteer explained with a widening big grin. "The dining room had a surplus of pumpkin pie from dinner the other night. Rather than spend the money for doughnuts, we thought it would be easier to take the extra pumpkin pie and serve it one more time. Tis the season for pumpkin pie, you know?"

"Yes," Bess replied, feeling her stomach turn at the prospect of eating pie for breakfast. "I think I'll just have a cup of coffee, thank you."

With those words, Bess grabbed a small cup of coffee and took a few sips. She could feel her body grow warm with each gulp. When she finished, she slipped on her coat and made her way towards the door. She couldn't help but notice that the line for voting had grown twice as long as it was when she first came. As she stepped outside to begin her walk home, a young man dressed in a dark suit opened the door for her.

"Thank you," Bess said.

"My pleasure," the man replied, and he quickly pulled out a bundle of flyers that he was carrying and shoved one paper in her hand. "Don't forget to vote, ma'am."

"But I..." Bess started to say but, before she could finish, the man handed her a flyer and quickly turned to the next person he could find.

She looked at the flyer. What she found was a series of smiling faces and names that made up a collective party of candidates urging her for support. Candidates for local, state, and federal offices smiled at her from the flyer. Bess let her eyes glide over the faces of these hopeful candidates of men and women seeking her vote. Then her eyes stopped at one candidate whose face looked vaguely familiar.

"I know you," she whispered to herself. She shook her head in disbelief at the man's face that grinned up at her from the paper. She folded the flyer and slipped it into her coat pocket, with a clear idea of what she was going to do with it.

Chapter 23: THE RASCAL

The next morning, Bess arrived for another meeting of her Bridge Club. For the first time in weeks, she wasn't carrying any grief or sadness to share with her friends. Instead the feeling she brought to the table was one of anger.

"Ladies, I've got a rascal to show you," she announced to her friends the very second she stepped into the Game Room of the main building. Flo, Alma, and Rose were seated around a table, cards dealt, waiting for Bess to join them. Instead, Bess tossed the political flyer onto the table, which sent some cards fluttering to the floor.

"Watch it!" Flo snapped and she quickly reached down to scoop up the cards. Alma and Rose looked confused over why Bess had dropped a political flyer at the center of the table. Once Flo had returned to the table with the stray cards, Bess pointed her finger down on one of the faces on the flyer.

"Ladies, do you see that face?" Bess asked. "Take a good look at the face I'm pointing at. *That* is a rascal!"

"Which one?" Flo giggled as she sat back down in her chair. "They're all politicians. They all look like rascals to me. Which rascal are we talking about?"

"Do you remember when I told you all about that stranger I found on the train?" Bess asked. "The one who was cheating on his wife? Well, that's him."

Suddenly, Alma and Rose stood up and leaned across the table to get a better look at the face that Bess was pointing at. Even Flo paused from shuffling her cards to glance over, then started shuffling the cards again. Rose reached over, picked up the flyer, and held it close enough to her face so her bifocals could work a little better.

"It says his name is . . ." Alma read.

"Don't say it!" Bess shouted and she pulled her finger away from the face and shook her head. "I read his name. I know what it is....I just don't want to hear it spoken."

"Aren't you touchy this morning?" Flo grinned.

"Certainly not," Bess quickly replied.

"I bet it's because he lied to you," Flo said in a soft voice. "I think you're mad because that fella lied to you and you didn't catch him telling a fib. Don't feel bad, Bess. Politicians can lie with the best of them."

"Suckered," Bess clarified. "I got suckered into believing his story about why he was cheating on his wife. Out there in California on business? Building some plant and falling in love with a young woman who owns a winery? Even the part where he said she reminded him of his wife when she was younger. For all I know, it could have just been his campaign manager he was fooling around with, not some vineyard owner. I chose to believe the romantic side...but another part of me should have known better."

"I wonder if he won or not?" Alma asked.

"I checked the morning paper before I came," Bess stated. "It did say he runs his own company. It also said he lost in his bid for a state senate seat."

"Leaving the state for California...I can see why he lost his election," Rose replied. "He should have been about campaigning instead of seeing his girlfriend."

"He's probably not upset that he lost," Bess said. "Now he'll have more time for his girlfriend...if that's what he was doing in California."

"I think you're lucky he lost, Bess," Alma said.

"What do you mean?" Bess asked, a little confused.

"I agree with Alma," Flo spoke up and her eyes turned to Bess. "You knew about his fling out in California, Bess. You'd be sitting on some juicy gossip if he were a senator."

"If he'd won the election, what would you have done with that fact?' Alma asked. "Gone to the newspapers? Made a big stink about what you knew about him?"

"Bess wouldn't make a 'big stink,' would you?" Rose chimed in.

Bess carefully folded up the flyer and dropped it in a trash container.

"He was very clever," Bess mumbled. "When he told me what I wanted to know, I think he knew he was confessing to the right sort of person."

"And what kind of person would that be?' Alma asked.

"Someone with the right background," Bess said a little louder and she tapped the top of the table with her hand. "If I were twenty years old, in college, and attractive...I don't think he would have been so honest. You see, ladies, I told him I was living in a retirement home. I told him my suspicions and I think he looked at my age, the place where I lived, and determined I was safe enough to convey his transgressions too. He knew that no one would believe an old lady from a retirement home."

"What makes you say that?" Rose asked.

"It's the same old story, ladies," Bess sighed and she looked around the table. "My age is the reason why I wouldn't have been believed. I think he told me those things because he knew a little old lady who lived in a retirement home wouldn't get much attention from the press. He knew that news reporters would only laugh if I told them my suspicions about the infidelities of a state senator. They would dismiss me straight away as being confused because of my age. Besides, I had no evidence to back up my story. So, I suppose I would have remained silent on the subject."

"Men!" Flo grunted. "You know when they started inventing those funny blue pills, it was the start of their problems. It's like giving a pill to a pig to make him eat more."

"Not all men are pigs," Alma gently offered.

"Of course, we're not talking about your Paul," Rose said.

"Yes," Bess nodded. "It just amazes me that this man can travel around, commit these transgressions, then feel entitled enough to run for public office! It takes a lot of nerve, if you ask me."

"And a lot of blue pills," Flo giggled.

"Well," Rose sighed. "I'd suppose there's nothing we can do about it now. The elections are over and that man can go back to his wife...or his girlfriend...whoever will take him."

With that notion, Bess picked up her cards and began thinking about the first round of bridge that was about to begin. As the game unfolded, the cards were played and more pleasant topics of conversation were exchanged. Bess smiled and laughed at the stories she heard. She savored the simple pleasures that filled the hour. She was grateful for the honesty and the companionship that came with her friendships. She was grateful that such honesty was a part of her life.

Chapter 24: GARDENING INTERRUPTED

Gardening in mid-October was for optimists. Bess told herself this more than once. On an unusually warm morning, she was reminded of this phrase while she decided to collect her gardening tools, step into the backyard, and begin the process of cleaning out her garden.

She found that her gardens provided her with a pleasant distraction from the mourning she still carried in her heart for Donald. At this point in the year, there were signs that the cooler nights were taking a toll on her vegetable garden. Some plants had turned brown. Some weeds had died. Still, there were plenty of signs of life to tend to.

She was amazed to find some full green zucchini ready to be plucked. She took a firm grip on the vegetable and pulled it from its stems. She also spotted a few ruby red tomatoes that appeared ready to be picked.

"A little late in the season for gardening!" a voice called out.

Bess looked up and was surprised to see a woman standing in her backyard, close to the edge of the garden. The woman, whom Bess did not recognize, appeared to be about ten years younger. She was short and round in such a way that it was difficult to determine where her stomach ended and her waist began. Her hair was a mix of gray and black. It was short and parted down the middle, falling just over her ears. When Bess stood up, she quickly noticed how the woman's dark hair offered a perfect fashion complement to her black slacks and her sky blue blouse.

"I love gardening no matter what time of the year," Bess said. "Do I know you?"

"I'm looking for someone named Bess Bullock," the woman answered and she glanced down at a small slip of paper in her hand. Watching a stranger read her name off a scrap of paper piqued Bess's curiosity.

"That would be me," Bess answered and she pointed to the woman's hand. "I can't help but notice that you're reading my name off a slip of paper. Did someone write down my name and address for you?"

"A friend of my mother's gave it to me," the woman replied. "My mom is a resident at the Honey Hills Center."

"And who is your mother?" Bess asked.

"Eveline Green," the woman replied. She then cleared her throat and took her nervously fidgeting hands and crossed them in front of her chest. "My name is Audrey Green. Eveline is my mother. I'm sorry for surprising you like this. It looks like you're in the middle of something. Maybe I should come back another time."

"No, no, excuse my manners. Please stay," Bess said and she brushed her hands together while she stepped out of her garden. "I'm a little dirty so do forgive me for my appearance. I know summer is over but I still have a few things in my garden to tend to."

Bess looked around. Her eyes lingered on the red tomatoes she was about to pick, then turned back to her guest.

"Another time," Bess whispered to the tomato before stepping out of her garden. She brushed the dirt from her hands and led Audrey to the back porch. Bess couldn't believe how brown her hands had become and rubbed them together again.

"You don't have to get cleaned up for me," Audrey commented. "It's fine if you've got dirt on your hands. I'm not a real high maintenance girl myself. I stopped worrying about that years ago when I got married."

"Yes, vanity and youth do seem to go hand in hand," Bess nodded as they reached the porch. She gestured to a pair of chairs. "Please sit down. Tell me why you're here."

"Isn't this quaint?" Audrey grinned before sitting down. She looked around at the yard, the garden and Bess could sense the scenery helped her to relax. "It's nice that they have places like this for folks like you to stay. I wish mom could have her own house, but she seems happy living in the main building. Your yard is so lovely."

"Yes, my husband and I are lucky to have our house and our yard to tend," Bess nodded. "During the summer, this is where we like to end the day…on our back porch. When the air is cool enough, we settle into these chairs and watch the sunset fill the sky with the kind of colors you'd expect from a child who has a box full of crayons."

"Sounds lovely," Audrey smiled.

"It is," Bess sighed. She shifted her chair over to get a better angle of Audrey's face.

"Well, you're not here to talk about sunsets. I must say I don't know your mother all that well. I know Eveline has been a resident since before I moved here. I've seen her in church on Sundays. She's just one of those familiar faces I've gotten used to seeing around the retirement center."

"That doesn't surprise me," Audrey answered. "Mom's been here for about five years. Now the woman who gave me your name, my mother's friend, she says you might be able to help me with something. She said you're like that. She told me you're good at helping the residents around here with their problems."

"And what problem do you have, my dear?" Bess asked.

"My mother simply won't leave the retirement home," Audrey answered. Her eyes dropped down to her lap. "To be more accurate, she won't leave...with me."

Audrey's eyes remained locked on her lap and Bess could see her eyes blink a little faster in what she guessed was an attempt to control some emotions.

"I'm sorry to hear that," Bess quietly offered. "Are you two having an argument?"

"No," Audrey quickly answered. She turned her eyes out to the yard. "A few weeks ago, my mother was always excited to come to my house for dinner or a visit. Then, one day, she decided she didn't want to come with me anymore."

"I see," Bess nodded and she adjusted her glasses, which were sliding down the slope of her nose. "I know many residents who fall into that situation. They are good people who simply become too comfortable with living here. When they become comfortable, they simply don't want to leave the main building anymore. For some it's how old age creeps into the mind I suppose."

"I can assure you that my mother has a sharp mind," Audrey began. "When I used to come around for her, she'd be standing outside waiting for me to take her away. The second she got in my car she had a big smile on her face. She so looked forward to doing things with me. Then one day....it happened."

"What?" Bess pressed.

"As I told you, one day I went to her room to pick her up and take her out for lunch. When I got to her room, she simply refused to come along," Audrey recalled. She turned her eyes from the yard and looked right at Bess. "At first, she said she wasn't feeling well. Then another day, the story changed to something about helping a friend with a project. Every time I'd try to take her some place, she had a reason not to go. The bottom line is that she simply refuses to leave her room with me, Mrs. Bullock, and I'm not quite sure why."

Audrey's voice began to quiver at the end of her statement. She wiped one eye with the back of her hand. Bess wanted to reach out and give her a hug, but with soil all over her fingers she felt it best to not offer any consolation.

"I must be honest," Bess finally began. "If your mother doesn't want to go somewhere, she certainly is entitled to make that choice. There's nothing I can do to force her to think otherwise."

"She comes out of her room," Audrey continued. "I've been told by one of her friends that mom is still leaving her room with her friends. She'll go for walks with them. In fact, I've heard she stepped out to attend a picnic just the other week. So why will she go out with her friends but not her own daughter? It really is upsetting to me. My mother doesn't want to spend time with me and I want to know why?"

"It's a reasonable question to ask," Bess said.

"My mother is very old," Audrey whispered. "I only have so much time to spend with her, Mrs. Bullock. She's not getting any younger. I want that time to be special….not spent sitting in a small room with her."

"I understand," Bess nodded. Her eyes narrowed and she looked at her garden. Her best ideas tended to come when she worked in her garden and she hoped that one would leap out of the garden and strike her. "You certainly have presented me with a curious problem,

Audrey. Again, I'm not quite certain what I can do to help."

"I think you should befriend my mother," Audrey explained. "I think you should befriend her to see if she will confide in you. My mother's a pretty chatty person. I think she'd talk to you once she got to know you. Maybe she'd even tell you what's keeping her from being with me. Maybe she'd tell you her reason for why she's treating me this way."

Bess took a deep breath and looked up at the sky. She could sense the desperation in Audrey's voice. When she looked at her, the expression on Audrey's face also conveyed a sense of hope that Bess would have a perfect solution. For a few seconds, she thought of her brother and the limited time he had left with his family. Time was fleeting and precious, Bess thought. She looked at Audrey and smiled.

"I'll help you, my dear," Bess quietly pointed out. "I just want to be very honest with you. I cannot magically get someone to reveal things to me if they don't wish to share them. I can only listen to the things that she *wants* to share. There's no guarantee that I will be successful. I want to make that perfectly clear. Do you understand?"

"I do," Audrey said.

"Then I'll do what I can," Bess said, standing up. "Now if you'd excuse me, I need to pick some tomatoes. We're going to have a chilly night tonight and I don't want to lose something to an early frost."

With those words, Bess made her way back to her garden. Audrey followed her to the garden, offering Bess her thanks again before leaving. With the sun settling into the horizon, and the sky turning violet, Bess stepped into her garden and began her last harvest by picking that one red tomato that had caught her eye earlier.

After scouring the garden for some more tomatoes, one cucumber, and a few carrots, Bess paused and glanced up to the peach colored sky. She drew in her breath and reflected on what she'd just agreed to. She thought about winning Eveline Green's trust. She thought about the many reasons why a mother would want to avoid the company of her own daughter. As a former police officer, her mind was intrigued at the possibilities for why Eveline was acting the way she was. As a mother, her heart ached for Audrey.

A few minutes later, Bess had left her garden carrying a small basket of vegetables. She walked over to the porch, sat down in her chair and allowed herself a moment to linger in the evening ambience that had gathered in her backyard.

"Did you find anything to pick?" Chet asked, stepping outside.

"A few things," Bess sighed.

The crickets chirped. The sky turned a deeper shade of scarlet. The fireflies emerged and danced with points of light. Bess looked at the beauty of the evening, drew in her breath and soaked it all in.

Are you thinking of Donald?" Chet asked, sitting down in the chair beside her.

"A little," Bess sighed.

"Some evenings when we watch the sunset, I don't know quite what you're thinking about," Chet said.

"Some nights it's about Donald," Bess replied. "Some nights I'm just thinking about a little mystery that's caught my eye."

"Grieving is a lonely thing," Chet sighed. "We're both widows. We've both lost family over the years. I've always thought of mourning as this long dance. The only problem is mourning has the lead and it decides when the dance is over."

"I'm still dancing, Chet," Bess nodded.

They sat quietly together. They watched the sky grow dark. They heard the crickets begin to chirp. They could feel that the day had quietly tucked itself away. Chet walked into the house while Bess remained on the deck to think about death and a new mystery.

Chapter 25: MAYBE A SHUT-IN

The next day Bess ventured into the main building
of the Honey Hills Center for a meeting of the Bridge
Club. When she reached the Game Room, she found
two of her friends had already arrived. Rose Grumbine
and Flo Morgenstern were seated at the table talking
about a mutual friend who had a run of good luck the
previous night playing bingo. When they spotted Bess,
Flo began to shuffle the cards and the topic of
conversation turned to the Pumpkin Parade and how it
was fast approaching. Alma Crisp entered the room a
few minutes later and soon another meeting of the
Bridge Club was ready to begin.

"I'm quite excited about this Pumpkin Parade," Rose
began. "It's about time we do something different
around here. I love Honey Hills, but sometimes a
change of pace is nice."

"I agree," Alma responded.

"How many pumpkins do you think we'll see?" Flo
asked.

"Fifty-one is what I heard," Rose replied.

"Really?" Alma laughed. "That many?"

"I wonder if they'll all be lit up or just decorated?"
Flo asked.

"A little of both...from what I've heard," Rose
answered.

"Bess, I can't wait to see what you and Chet did with
your pumpkin," Alma said.

Bess was slow to respond. While she knew that
Chet's clown pumpkin would make for entertaining

conversation, her thoughts were occupied with Audrey Green's most unusual request.

"Bess?" Alma said, her voice growing louder. "Are you listening to us?"

"I'm sorry," Bess began, waving her hand in the air. "While I'm looking forward to the pumpkin parade, I have other things on my mind this morning."

"Are you still grieving for your brother?" Rose asked.

"That...and I had a most unusual visitor stop by my house yesterday," Bess stated. "A very nice lady who interrupted my gardening. She was distraught about how her mother doesn't want to spend time with her anymore. Her mother is a resident here. Her name is Eveline Green?"

"I know Eveline," Rose quickly responded. "She's a shut-in."

"No, she isn't," Alma said, and her head quickly turned to Rose. "I just saw her at bingo last week. She looked quite happy playing and chatting with the ladies at her table. I don't think you're a shut-in when you do things like that."

"I agree," Bess nodded, and she leaned forward a little and looked across the table at Rose. "I see her in church every Sunday, too. So why did you call her a shut-in, Rose?"

Rose began to shuffle a deck of cards and deal them out without a reply.

"Because of something I overheard," Rose finally answered.

"You always eavesdrop," Flo mumbled.

"That's how she gets good gossip," Alma giggled.

"Well, this wasn't too hard to overhear," Rose began. "The other week I was walking back to my room after breakfast when I heard a woman's voice speaking quite loudly to someone. Listening to what was being said, I thought it was a mother of a child. When I rounded the corner to a hallway, the voice grew louder and sharper. Then I spotted a short dark-haired woman standing just outside of a resident's room addressing someone inside the room with a stern voice and a finger that she jabbed at the air. Like I said before, I thought it was a parent addressing a temperamental child. When I got closer, I realized it wasn't a child being scolded…it was Eveline Green being lectured to by her daughter."

"What did you hear her say?" Bess asked.

"I don't recall the exact words," Rose replied. "If I remember correctly, the issue was that Eveline was refusing to go out to lunch with her daughter. Eveline said she wasn't hungry. The daughter then offered to take her shopping, but Eveline again expressed her desire to stay in her room. Apparently, this has happened before, or so I heard the daughter mention. After overhearing all of that, it led me to think that Eveline was simply going to stay in her room and never come out. You know, some residents get like that when they've lived here for a while."

"And you know what happens after that," Flo stated. "The nurses try to coax you out and when they can't…they take you to the dementia wing. I've seen that happen to ladies in my hallway. It's not pretty, I can tell you that—lots of yelling when they drag them out of their rooms."

"Well, Eveline leaves her room," Bess observed. "Whether it be for church or bingo or even her meals in the Dining Hall. We've all seen her around the building."

Rose nodded at the comments.

"I suppose those are all good points," Rose sighed. "And yet, from what I overheard her daughter say, Eveline simply is refusing to go anywhere with her.

Why would someone refuse to leave this place with their own child?"

"Mothers and daughters," Alma sighed. "My mother and I always clashed over clothes. She just wasn't a fancy dresser, like me."

"None of us are," Flo giggled.

"I think you're right, Rose," Bess nodded. "Why would anyone refuse to leave here with their own child? Why would they turn their child away?"

The question hung in the air without an answer. All three ladies looked back at their cards and began playing another round of bridge. Bess eventually let her mind focus on the game and her own cards. Yet, in the back of her mind, questions about Eveline's problem lingered.

Chapter 26: PRAYERS AND PATIENCE

When Sunday arrived, Bess and Chet were in their usual morning routines to prepare for church. Chet rose first, earlier than on a weekday, and dressed in his best navy blue suit and matching tie. Bess slipped on a lavender dress with a gold necklace and matching earrings. When they met in the kitchen, there was no time for their usual leisurely breakfast. Two bowls of oatmeal and two glasses of juice were quickly consumed before it was time to leave for church. Given that she always wore her best shoes to church, it was the one day out of the week that Chet was happy to drive to the main building.

When they arrived, Bess and Chet followed the stream of residents through the hallways that led to the sanctuary in the main building. Bess preferred to sit on the right side of the church, where the windows caught the morning sun. Upon entering the church, Chet instinctively turned right and began to head for their usual pew. Bess grabbed him by the arm, causing Chet to turn with a confused expression.

"Wait," Bess said. She stood in the back of the church, looking around at the other residents in attendance. There were many white and gray heads to scan. Then, in a section to the left of the altar, Bess managed to spot Eveline Green sitting in a pew by herself.

"The service is about to begin," Chet said, looking around at the church with a look of slight panic on his face. "Bess? Did you hear me?"

"Come this way," Bess quickly replied, discreetly waving Chet to follow her. The music began to play and Bess could feel the eyes that were following them up a side aisle.

She led Chet to the pew where Eveline was seated by herself.

When they stepped into the pew, Bess was careful to glance over to Eveline and offer her a polite smile before sitting down. Bess slid a little closer to Eveline, but not too close so as to raise suspicions. Once the distance was right, Bess turned to Chet and spoke to him in a soft voice about something trivial. With this action, she hoped to give Eveline the impression that she was only choosing the pew to have a better view of the service.

As the service commenced, Bess entertained her mind with a variety of ways to engage Eveline in conversation. The subjects swirled in her head, creating a level of distraction that even she was embarrassed by. Only Bess and God knew how little she was focusing on this morning's scripture reading and she felt badly for it.

Eventually, she managed to listen to the sermon. It was a homily on faith, the power of not going through life holding onto facts to dismiss using faith. Life required faith to help in times when the facts weren't known. From what she heard, Bess began to understand the very subtle differences between believing in facts and believing in faith. Sometimes in life, believing in the truth required faith. Knowing the facts required one to exercise little faith. As a former police officer, not knowing the facts went against everything Bess believed in. As was the case with any good sermon, it gave her something to challenge her beliefs. Eventually, the minister went on to draw an analogy.

"When you run into an old friend," the minister began, "there is little faith required to exercise that old friendship. You already know the facts that make up that person and those facts make you comfortable. In contrast, when you meet a person for the first time, you take a leap of faith in trying to get to know them better. That is when faith comes into our hearts. It is that driving force that leads us to get to know an acquaintance better. It leads us to make new friends and new friendships. When you leave here today, exercise your faith. Get to know someone better."

Bess smiled at the message and hoped that Eveline was also listening to it.

Soon the last hymn was sung and the service drew to a close. Bess placed her hymnal into the holder and turned to Eveline. She smiled and Eveline offered a smile back.

"Good morning," Bess grinned. "My name is Bess Bullock."

"Eveline Green," she replied and she offered a measured smile after speaking.

'I thought that was a beautiful sermon," Bess sighed as she followed Eveline into the main aisle. "Faith is such a tricky thing to manage in this world. I can pray to God in the morning, and then I find myself making all kinds of demands of my daughter. Demands I probably shouldn't make."

By mentioning her daughter, Bess felt she was off to a quick start in trying to find common ground with Eveline.

"Yes," Eveline nodded. "I agree. Faith is a tricky thing."

"Do you have any children?" Bess asked. "Sometimes, even though she is grown, my daughter can still test my faith and my good nature as a mother."

"Yes, I have a daughter," Eveline replied. "I can't really say that she tests me in any way. I love her more than she'll ever know. We're two pairs of the same heart."

Bess smiled at the response. In a few words, she had offered the mutual topic of motherhood to discuss with Eveline. She had also successfully established some comfort with Eveline in the fact that they both had daughters.

"That's nice to hear," Bess answered. "You're quite lucky, Eveline. Quite lucky indeed to have a daughter so much like yourself."

"I think we're both lucky, Bess," Eveline smiled. "A mother is a lucky thing to be."

With those words, Bess turned to Chet and quickly introduced him to Eveline. Then Chet took Bess by the hand and together they began to exit the pew. Bess turned back to Eveline and thought about the nicest way to say goodbye.

"It really was very nice to meet you, Eveline Green," Bess said. "I hope we see each other again. Maybe we can talk more about our daughters."

"I think I'd enjoy that," Eveline answered and the expression on her face told Bess that the words were a true reflection from her heart.

Bess followed Chet out of the pew and down the main aisle. She looked back over her shoulder and smiled one more time at Eveline before leaving the sanctuary. She made eye contact with Eveline and they exchanged one more smile. As she and Chet walked to their car, Bess felt good about what had just happened. In a quick conversation, she had managed to plant some seeds of friendship in Eveline's heart. She hoped that those seeds would grow.

Chapter 27: NURTURING AN ACQUAINTANCE

Time. If there was one thing that Bess needed in order to establish a close relationship with Eveline, it was time. Since her pleasant chat with Eveline in church, Bess found herself spending more and more time in the main building with hopes of seeing Eveline again. Of course, she couldn't simply walk into her room and start chatting. The encounters had to be subtler. Passing in the hallways, eating lunch in the Dining Hall at the same time and attending the same programs were just some of the ways Bess was able to encounter Eveline.

On those occasions when she was fortunate enough to cross paths with Eveline, Bess would offer a warm smile and a few kind words to remind Eveline of their previous conversation in church and their love for the daughters. If they passed in the hallway, Bess would also make a point of greeting Eveline by name.

While she felt good about the number of times she was coming into contact with her subject, Bess knew that the smiles and brief exchanges were the stuff that made one an acquaintance and not a stranger. Passing in the halls or chatting after a program were nice, but Bess needed to have longer, more meaningful exchanges. She needed to be more than an acquaintance to win Eveline's trust. As her mother once told her, meaningful conversations are the soil from which good friendships grow.

As the days passed, Bess began to find more opportunities to see Eveline. She began to notice that if she walked by Eveline's room at certain times of the day, the door to her room was cracked just enough that Bess could look in to see Eveline watching TV or reading. When those opportunities came about, Bess began to step into the doorway, make eye contact with Eveline, and talk for a bit. Sometimes Eveline would even wave her in for a visit. It was another step, Bess thought, in getting to know Eveline better.

While she was focused on the question of the odd behavior Eveline showed towards her daughter, she was genuinely starting to enjoy the company of her subject. The more they spoke, the more Bess found it hard to remember that Eveline was avoiding her daughter. Eveline kept a busy schedule throughout the week. She had plenty of friends and plenty of social engagements. All in all, Bess found Eveline to be about as normal as any other resident of the Honey Hills Center.

One Sunday morning, after church, Bess lingered by Eveline's pew and chatted about how their day was going to unfold. It was a pleasant conversation, and with good feelings filling the air. Sensing the positive mood, Bess decided it was time to cut to the heart of the matter.

"My daughter is coming to take Chet and me out for lunch," Bess stated. She smiled after the comment and stepped closer to Eveline. "That's just our routine on Sundays. It's quite nice. The three of us and my granddaughter have a Sunday brunch and talk about our week. Do you ever do anything like that with your daughter?"

"Not as often as I used to," Eveline said, the smile slowly vanishing from her face.

"I suppose your daughter is too busy? I know my daughter's life is a whirlwind," Bess observed.

"My daughter's life isn't all that busy," Eveline quickly replied. "I'm afraid the whole situation is just....complicated."

Bess nodded and looked around at the residents filing out of the church. With the sanctuary all but empty, Eveline finally took a step into the main aisle and Bess slowly followed her towards the exit.

"Mothers and daughters are indeed quite complicated," Bess nodded. "That is such a shame, Eveline. You speak so fondly of her when we talk. It must be very frustrating for you not to go out with her for lunch. You know, lunch is my favorite meal of the day."

Eveline dipped her head down and forced a smile to the floor.

"My daughter is the sweetest person I know," Eveline observed. She paused for a few seconds then stopped walking. "Unfortunately, she does not have the best taste in men."

"Didn't you tell me once that your daughter was engaged?" Bess recalled.

"Yes," Eveline nodded. "She's going to have a husband soon. His name is Kenny."

"Does he treat your daughter nicely?' Bess asked. "You know, when you're young, passions can run deep. Tempers flare more when you're younger than when you're older. Does he show any kind of temper towards your daughter?"

"Not towards my daughter," Eveline replied.

Bess couldn't help but notice that after making that statement, Eveline took her left hand, reached over and rolled up the sleeve to her lavender blouse. What Bess saw was completely unexpected.

Eveline's arm was marked by a bright yellow spot that looked like an oval. Inside the oval were deep maroon blotches. The bruise appeared to be the size of a hand that grabbed hold of her arm too tightly.

"Oh my," Bess sighed and she covered her mouth with her hand.

Eveline quickly turned down her sleeve, her eyes darting around at some residents lingering just ahead of them.

"It looks worse than what it is," Eveline quietly explained. "You see I take blood thinner. As a result, I bruise easily and it takes longer for the bruises to go away."

"When did you get this ugly mark?" Bess asked.

"A few weeks ago," Eveline replied. "I was at my daughter's house for dinner with her and her fiancé, Kenny. My daughter went to the store to pick up some ice cream for desert. While she was away, Kenny and I were cleaning up after dinner. We started to disagree over something trivial. At my age, I recognize trivial when I see it. The argument was about cleaning up after dinner. Kenny preferred to place things in the sink for my daughter to rinse later. I thought it would be more helpful to rinse them off and then put them in the dishwasher. It was a small disagreement on how to do things."

"At our age many disagreements appear small," Bess nodded.

"Now Kenny is a good man," Eveline continued, "but he does have a quick temper. When I tried to talk to him about doing it my way, we bickered for a minute. Then he took a firm grip on my arm, pushed me to the side and filled the sink with dirty dishes. It was all quite uncomfortable. When my daughter returned from the store, she quickly came to my defense. Kenny yelled at her. Eventually everything did calm down, but I haven't been back to my daughter's home since."

There it was, Bess thought. The mystery about Eveline and her *shut-in* behavior was suddenly revealed. The secret behind her actions came out as matter-of-factly as the sun appears from behind a cloud. The intimacy that Bess had nurtured between herself and Eveline had finally paid off.

"Well," Bess began. "You're more than welcome to join us for lunch today."

"Thank you, Bess," Eveline replied. "I don't want to impose."

Together both ladies walked down the main aisle. Chet stood at the back of the church, waiting for them. He opened the door to the sanctuary for both ladies to exit, then followed them out into the hallway.

"Lovely service," Chet said.

"Yes, it was a lovely service and a lovely morning," Eveline replied.

"I was trying to persuade Eveline to join us for brunch," Bess said.

"I don't want to be a third wheel," Eveline mumbled.

"Nonsense," Chet replied. "The only kind of wheels I find annoying are the squeaky kind. I insist you come with us."

"Yes," Bess nodded. "There's a coffee shop about five minutes from here. They make home-made doughnuts, which my granddaughter loves. They also make the best Belgian waffles, which I have with fresh strawberries."

"Are the strawberries still fresh this far into autumn?" Eveline asked.

"I don't ask," Bess laughed. "All I know is that they're juicy and sweet and they make me smile when I eat them."

"They sound delightful!" Eveline said.

"Well, they're just five minutes away," Chet grinned. "All you have to do is come with us. Bess's daughter will pick us up and we'll all have a wonderful breakfast."

"You make it sound so simple," Eveline laughed.

"Sometimes the good things in life are like that—simple," Bess observed.

She reached out and took Eveline's hand. Together the three of them walked out of the small chapel, out of the Honey Hills Center, and off to a place of for a morning of Belgian waffles, strawberries and laughter.

Chapter 28: THE PROBLEMS WITH SOLUTIONS

"So poor Eveline was abused?" Flo nodded from behind her cards. "You know I read an article that talked about how older people like us can be hurt and abused by family members. The article said that most victims feel that they should just take the abuse and not report it. I'm so glad that Eveline told you."

"It is a shame," Rose chimed in. "Especially when it's family committing the abuse."

"He's not family yet," Bess pointed out. "He's only the fiancé."

"A technicality," Flo added. "I don't care if he's the King of France. No one has the right to grab an elderly woman by the arm and leave a nasty bruise. Saying he's almost family sounds like you're giving him an excuse for what he did."

"There's another problem," Bess paused for a moment and looked around the table. "Now I face the difficult task of telling Audrey Green that her mother is too afraid of her fiancé to leave the Honey Hills Center with her. I don't think anyone wants to hear news like that."

"Maybe it will be a wake up call for her," Alma observed. "I mean, when you're about to marry someone…it's hard to think about all the qualities you're going to be living with. They're qualities you'll be sharing for a lifetime."

"Are you speaking from experience?" Flo asked.

"Not at all," Alma answered. "I loved my husband with all my heart, God rest his soul. Now I love my fiancé, too. Paul is a good man. He'd never think of grabbing me that hard."

"I like Paul," Bess spoke up. "I enjoyed talking to him. I couldn't imagine him hurting you, Alma."

"So now that you know the truth, what are you going to do?" Rose asked.

"I guess I just need to take a deep breath, look Audrey in the eye and have a difficult conversation," Bess sighed.

Chapter 29: TRUTH

The next day, Bess called Audrey and told her she had some news. Later in the afternoon, Audrey swung by the house. After some pleasantries, Bess suggested they move out to the back porch, since Audrey commented on how much she liked the setting from her previous visit. It was another unusually warm day for autumn, but the sun was angled in just the right way to cast a stroke of shade across the back porch. As she led Audrey out to the porch and settled in her chair, Bess wasn't sure if she was sweating because of the weather or because she was nervous about the conversation she was about to have.

"Thank you for calling," Audrey began. "You said you had something to share about my mother?"

"I do," Bess nodded. "The good news is that your plan worked. Your mother and I have gotten to know each other quite well over the last few weeks. As you said, she's a very kind person. She also enjoys talking, so we really have hit it off. I think we're going to be good friends."

Audrey merely smiled and nodded at Bess's words.

"During one of our discussions, she told me why she won't leave with you," Bess announced.

"Why?" Audrey asked, leaning forward in her seat, her mouth slowly opening like she was about to consume something sweet and juicy.

Bess thought about the truth and considered her words carefully.

"Tell me about your fiancé," Bess began.

"Kenny?" Audrey asked and her eyebrows dropped. "Is that why she won't come to see me? Is it because of Kenny? Did he yell at her? I told him to be nice."

"Do you remember the last time you had your mother to your house for dinner?" Bess asked.

"Yes, I think so," Audrey nodded.

"It was a dinner when you stepped out to the store for ice cream," Bess continued. "Did she tell you that she and Kenny got into a disagreement while they were cleaning up after dinner? The argument culminated when he grabbed her by the arm with such force that it left a bruise. Now I'm certain he didn't mean to hurt her, but when people are upset they do tend to let their emotions escalate until they get…physical."

"Kenny is a kind man," Audrey explained and she looked out towards Bess's garden. "I…I know he has a rough side to him sometimes, but he'd never hurt me. I've been with him for four years and while he can be loud and have strong opinions, he's never been abusive to anyone that I'm aware of. I just don't think he knew how hard he grabbed her arm."

"Be that as it may," Bess said, her eyes turning out to her yard, "that is the reason why she won't go with you anymore. I think her fear of Kenny is keeping her in the safety of our retirement home."

Audrey's eyes turned to her lap where her hands were cupped together, as if she she were about to pray. She drew in her breath and turned to Bess.

"So what do I do?" Audrey asked. "I love my mother…but I also love Kenny."

"That is a difficult choice," Bess agreed.

"I shouldn't have to choose," Audrey sighed.

"You once told me you wanted to spend time with your mother outside of her room," Bess recalled. "Why not tell her a little white lie. Every daughter has told her mother a lie now and then. Tell her that Kenny is out of town before you offer to take her out. Maybe you simply need to tell her it's a ladies day out. Find some excuse that will put her mind at ease about Kenny and I think she'll be more receptive to your invitations."

"I wish it were that easy," Audrey sighed. "She's a mother. She knows when I'm fibbing to her."

"I see," Bess nodded. "Well, you asked me to find you a reason for your mother's actions. A solution is an altogether different matter."

"You're right," Audrey nodded. "It's my problem to solve. Thank you so much."

With those words, Audrey stood up and stepped off the porch. She stepped into the yard and quietly headed to the street where her car was parked. Bess got out of her chair, stepped off the porch, and followed Audrey through the grass and into the front yard.

"You know it's not your fault!" Bess called out.

"What?" Audrey replied, stopping at the curb to the street. Bess made her way across her yard and stepped in front of Audrey.

"There's never a simple solution in life," Bess stated. "Life is like…a hand sewn quilt. If one stitch is off in the quilt, a good deal of the lining must be removed to repair it. A simple problem can be a complex thing when making a quilt. I've often thought that life never gives us problems that we can simply nip off like a loose thread. Life gives us problems that are subtle and nuanced and not easily solved. That's why it's not your fault. It's just how life is…at least that's been my experience."

Audrey smiled.

"Well, I don't know how this problem will be solved, but you're right, Mrs. Bullock. If a solution can be found it must be a complicated one," Audrey replied.

She turned and stepped into the street and got into her car. Bess followed behind Audrey, her mind racing for a solution as to how she could get her mother to come out of her room. The issue at hand seemed to be Eveline's familiarity with Audrey bending the truth. Any mother would have a lifetime of cues in reading her daughter before catching her in a lie; the expression on her face, how her eyes widen or narrow, how the tone in her voice changes or where her eyes look.

As Audrey climbed into her car, Bess glanced across the street at one of her neighbors. She watched as the neighbor spread rabbit repellent around the edge of her garden. Bess was quite familiar with that brand of repellent, having used it herself on her vegetable garden. The image of watching this neighbor spread the repellent brought a curious smile to Bess's face. A warm feeling washed over her the way it usually did when she had a good idea.

"I think I may have a solution," Bess grinned and she stepped up to the open window of the car.

What followed were wise words regarding a strategy to solve the problem. The look on Audrey's face was one of tension and worry. The longer Bess spoke, she could see Audrey's worried expression begin to melt into a smile. Bess smiled too. Both ladies agreed they may have found a full proof way to get Audrey out of her room.

Chapter 30: CONCLUSION

It was Tuesday morning and Bess sat in the Game Room with her Bridge Club, sharing the news of how the case of Eveline Green had ended.

"So what did you tell the daughter?" Alma asked.

"I told her what her mother confided in me...which was a fear of the fiancé," Bess stated.

"A well-founded fear, if you ask me," Rose chimed in.

"Yes," Flo nodded. "And after hearing all that, is the daughter still going to marry that rascal?"

"I think so," Bess said, rubbing her forehead. "Unfortunate as that is, I suppose we simply can't make the decisions we want to for our daughters. That young lady is making a terrible decision and her mother will simply have to endure it."

"So Eveline won't be leaving here with her daughter?" Alma asked.

"I shared an idea with Audrey and she thought it was a good one to get her mother to go with her," Bess grinned.

"And what idea was that?" Rose asked.

"I slipped Eveline a little something to bolster her confidence around Kenny," Bess smiled.

"What?" Alma asked.

"A small can of pepper spray," Bess giggled.

"Pepper spray?" Rose laughed.

"Good for you," Flo nodded.

"Where in the world did you get pepper spray?" Alma asked.

"It was something my daughter gave me a few years ago when I was living by myself," Bess explained. "It's a little container that fits on my keychain. Of course, I've never used it. I don't even know if it works. I just thought, something small like that would give Eveline the confidence she needs to leave this place with her daughter."

"But what if she uses it on the fiancé?" Alma asked.

"Then he probably deserves it," Flo shot back.

All the women around the table laughed in agreement.

"I got a call from Eveline's daughter yesterday," Bess continued. "She said she and her mother had a lovely lunch. She thanked me again for all of my help."

"All's well that ends well," Rose sighed.

Bess looked around the table and grinned at each of her friends.

"Confidence, ladies," Bess sighed. "Imagine what we all could do if we had that little extra confidence in ourselves. I think it's something we lose as we get older."

"How true," Alma chimed in. "I know if I had a bottle of it in my medicine cabinet I'd take a spoonful every morning."

"A spoonful of confidence wouldn't hurt anyone," Flo mumbled.

"I agree," Rose sighed.

After this observation, the table grew silent. Bess and her friends settled into their card game. It was a well played round of bridge. It was a round played with confidence.

Chapter 31: THE CALL

A phone call can change everything. By simply answering the phone, one entertains the very real possibility of learning something. It might be something as mundane as a confirmed date or appointment. It might be a phone call that elicits a smile or warm words from a friend. It might even be a call that takes everything in one's life and turns it upside down. Bess could easily recall the moment she'd answered the phone to learn of her brother's death. It had led her to a cross-country train ride and weeks of grief.

One morning, while Bess was reading the newspaper with Chet, she heard the phone ring. The second she reached for the phone, her expectations of another mundane phone call were at the forefront of her mind. That expectation quickly changed when she put the phone to her ear.

"Hello?" Bess said into the phone.

"Mrs. Bullock," a man's voice spoke.

"Yes," she answered.

"This is Casper Waynright," the voice answered followed by a long pause for Bess to respond. Bess had no idea who Casper Waynright was and she continued to wait for him to speak some more. "I'm the director of the Honey Hills Center. I doubt you remember me but we met briefly the year you and your daughter signed papers to move you into the Honey Hills Center."

"I remember," Bess quickly answered out of courtesy. She had a vague recollection of him but she really didn't recall any specific face to go with the name. "That was quite a long time ago, but it was a day I will always remember. When your child takes control of your life like that, it's something you don't easily forget."

This time it was Casper Waynright who paused at the other end of the phone.

"I understand," Waynright finally answered. "My reason for calling this morning is because I need your help with something. Would you be able to come over this morning to meet with me?"

"Well," Bess began, glancing out her kitchen window, "it looks like it's raining pretty hard. My husband and I don't like to drive on rainy days. It might be a bit too messy for me to walk there."

"I can send a shuttle to pick you up," Waynright offered. "How soon could you be ready?"

Bess could sense some urgency in his voice. She looked down at her slippers, her pajamas, and the dirty breakfast dishes stacked by the sink. She then glanced down at Chet who was working on a crossword puzzle. She thought about the phone call she was taking and her mind pondered a question.

"Am I in some kind of trouble?" Bess asked.

The question caused Chet to look up from his puzzle and put his pencil down.

"No, you're not," Waynright replied. "However, one of my nurses may be in a great deal of trouble. Legal trouble."

"I'm retired, Mr. Waynright," Bess explained. "I'm not a police officer anymore."

"But you still help people with problems," Waynright countered. "A few nurses tell me you've helped quite a few of our residents with their little dilemmas. I'm merely asking you to show me the same courtesy. Please let me send a shuttle to come and pick you up so I can share my problem with you."

Bess put the phone on her shoulder. While she liked keeping busy to take her mind off her grief, this was an all together different situation. The director of the nursing home was asking her for her help. Was she in a position to anger him by turning him down? She pulled the phone back up to her ear.

"Send me a shuttle in one hour," Bess said. "I'll be waiting."

When she hung up the phone, Bess looked down at the floor to reflect on everything that had just transpired with one phone call. Her eyes turned to Chet, who was sipping his coffee and studying his crossword puzzle again.

"What was that all about?' he asked, looking up at her.

"The director of the nursing home needs my help," Bess replied.

"Can I do anything to help?" Chet asked.

Bess nodded, her eye glancing around the kitchen before walking to the bedroom to change.

"Clean up those dirty dishes!" Bess called out from the bedroom.

Chapter 32: THE CURIOUS PAIN

The ride in the shuttle bus was a bit strange. Bess did not make it her habit to ride in the small retirement bus. In fact, the only time she used the service was if she and Chet were going into town for some shopping. On those occasions, there were other residents in the van to talk to and the mood was festive. Leaving the Honey Hills ground every once in a while for a change of scenery was a reason to celebrate. Yet, on this gray rainy morning, Bess was not feeling festive. She was the only person on the shuttle and the weather outside was terrible.

The engine rumbled and the rain splashed against the windows. As they left Dogwood Lane, she could hear the rain falling harder, sounding like marbles being dropped on the roof of the bus. She looked out the window at the gray day and sighed. The bus slowly moved down the street and turned onto Magnolia Lane, before accelerating towards the main building of the Honey Hills Center.

As the bus pulled up, Bess looked out the window where she saw a tall man dressed in a black suit, standing by the entrance to the building. His hair was dark, with streaks of gray along the sides. She also noted that the gray hair extended down the side of his face to a slight beard that ran around the bottom of his chin. His arms were folded across his chest and he appeared to be staring at the ground. When the bus drew closer, the man's arms dropped to his side and he walked right up to the curb.

"Thank you for the ride," Bess said to the driver before making her way off the bus. She carefully stepped out of the bus to where the overhang to the main entrance was located. The wind blew and some drops of rain struck her arm. She quickly stepped to where the man with the beard was waiting.

"I'm Casper Waynright. Thank you for coming, Mrs. Bullock," he said, and he reached out and took her hand and gently shook it. Then, as if to reinforce his self-importance, he quickly turned and stepped inside, leaving Bess to trail behind him.

As she followed him through the hallways, she found his pace brisk, challenging to keep up with. This early in the morning, her legs were unwilling to move faster to keep up with him, but she did her best. Eventually, he glanced over his shoulder and noticed how she was trailing behind.

"Nasty weather out there," he muttered and his strides finally slowed.

"Yes, it is," Bess replied.

"Now is it Mrs. Bullock or Mrs. Wooden?" Waynright asked, the tone in his voice growing higher. "I noticed in your file that you got married to another resident. Some nurses said you were Mrs. Wooden while others insisted I call you Mrs. Bullock. Which do you prefer?"

"I tried Mrs. Wooden," Bess confessed, "but it was just too much for me to remember my new last name. I guess after being a *Bullock* for sixty years, it's just too hard for me to change. My current husband is okay with me keeping my last name. It gives me one less thing to remember, which at my age is a blessing."

The little joke didn't cause Mr. Waynright to answer. While she followed him through the halls, Bess managed to smile at a few of the residents she knew. A couple of them shot her confused looks as she walked by. The expressions on the faces of some of the residents reminded Bess of being a schoolgirl and having the principal escort her off the playground.

"I feel like I'm about to be punished," Bess said.

"That's hardly the case," Mr. Waynright replied.

Soon they arrived at his office. They settled into a brown leather couch that had plenty of room for them to sit. Bess took a few seconds to catch her breath after the lengthy walk to his office.

"My, this is comfy," Bess sighed, running her hand over the cool leather.

"I've been known to sleep on this couch once or twice a month," Mr. Waynright stated with a sense of pride creeping into his voice.

"You've slept in your office?" Bess asked.

"In my position, sometimes I find it necessary," Mr. Waynright explained while he brushed a piece of fuzz from his pants leg. "The Honey Hills Center is a big facility. There are times when I need to stay over night just to walk around and make sure things are running smoothly on late shifts. Unfortunately, things have not been operating as I would like... which is why I called you."

"And why isn't it running smoothly?" Bess asked and she propped her elbow on the armrest and stroked the side of her head while she waited for a reply.

"We've had some complaints," Mr. Waynright began and he tapped his fingers on the arm of the couch. "Of course, we always listen to residents' suggestions about how we do things around here. However, this particular complaint was becoming a problem I simply couldn't ignore."

"And what was the complaint about?" Bess asked.

"Pain," Mr. Waynright simply answered. "The problem was pain."

"I'm sorry?" Bess asked, a bit confused by his answer.

"As you know, some of our residents suffer from various forms of discomfort," Mr. Waynright began. "Of course, this is no surprise. It's a part of the aging process. Some residents suffer from arthritis. Some have inflammation in their joints. We have quite a few patients whose pain we try to manage. Now, of course, we would freely pass out an anti-inflammatory to anyone who needs it. However, some of our residents have more profound discomfort. There are some residents who need the strongest pain relievers we can give them. Oxycodone is what we provide to those residents. Unfortunately, we haven't been able to provide it to enough of them."

"Why?" Bess asked.

"Every day our nurses' stations are allocated a specific amount of oxycodone for patients who need it. We really try to keep tight reins on how it is used because the drug is so addictive. Unfortunately, someone has been switching out our supply of oxycodone with aspirin," Waynright quickly answered. He stood up, walked over to the door to his office and closed it, then sat back down on the couch with Bess.

"How long has this been happening?" Bess asked.

"At first, some of the residents complained about discomfort," Waynright recalled. "We tried a variety of things to relieve it. After a while, we realized the root of the problem was coming from their medication. A few of them simply weren't getting the dose they needed. So now, we're left with the difficult situation of finding a staff member who's been taking the oxycodone. Unfortunately, we've been unable to figure out who it is."

"Why not call the police instead of me?" Bess asked. "If you have someone stealing drugs, I believe that's a matter for the authorities."

"I agree with you, Mrs. Bullock," Waynright nodded. "We *did* call the police. They came in and they did an investigation, but they couldn't find anyone to implicate."

"Why do you think that is?" Bess asked.

"Nothing was being stolen when they were around," Waynright explained. "Having uniformed officers here caused our thief to stop taking things. All of our patients got their meds and there were no complaints. When the police presence left, it started again with residents complaining of pain. The police then tried to have one of their own pretend to be a nurse, but the other nurses picked up on it pretty quickly. A new face on the day shift is easy to spot, plus the officer in question had no idea what she was doing."

"So you're suspecting a nurse is taking this...oxycodone?" Bess asked.

"Yes," Waynright replied. "Pills like that can be sold for a good price. High school kids would pay for them. It's very addicting medicine, Mrs. Bullock."

"And you think a nurse is doing this?" Bess asked.

"A nurse seems the most likely to suspect," Waynright said. "They're the only ones with access to it. They're around the meds all day. They could easily swap out an oxycodone with an aspirin and no one would notice...except a resident in pain."

"I see," Bess nodded and she tapped her hands on her lap and pondered the situation. "Well, there are many nurses who work here. How would you know where to begin?"

"We began to notice a pattern when we discovered it was happening," Waynright stated. "The complaints about pain seemed to be happening more in the evenings. That's when a good many of our patients were complaining about pain. Not a lot, but enough to draw attention to the problem."

"There are many nurse's stations in the main building," Bess pointed out. "How would you know where to begin?"

Mr. Waynright stood up and walked over to his desk. He then waved Bess to join him at the desk where he pointed out a piece of paper from his desk. He handed the paper to Bess. When she looked at it, she saw that it was a map of the main building. It appeared that someone had taken a red pen and circled a portion of the map. When Bess held the paper a little closer to her face, she saw that what was circled were residents' room numbers.

"These are the residents who had been complaining the most about their pain," Mr. Waynright stated. "I asked the nurses to record their names and room numbers. As you can see, the complaints fall around this particular station. There are a set number of nurses assigned to work at the station. These nurses are there every day. I suspect that one of them is the guilty party."

Bess stared at the room numbers on the paper, then looked up to Mr. Waynright.

"So what is it you'd like me to do?" she asked.

"As I mentioned," Waynright began. "The police officers were too obvious in their presence around that station. Even the one that tried to blend in as a nurse was picked out. I need a face the nurses are used to seeing. A face they won't suspect. I also need a pair of eyes who can roam around the center without drawing attention. From what I understand, you have a good way of watching things without being noticed."

"That may be true," Bess stated. "In speaking from experience, your nurses have a good eye for things. If they figured out an undercover police officer was in their midst, they could easily think the same thing of me."

"That's a chance I'm willing to take," Waynright said.

Bess stared down at the map again. She knew that this was a matter of grave importance and that any excuse she gave to avoid this invitation would not be accepted.

"May I keep this?" Bess asked, pointing to the map.

"I'll have my secretary make a copy for you," Mr. Waynright replied and he reached over and took it off his desk. "I realize you live on Dogwood Lane, Mrs. Bullock, but it would be beneficial if you could spend more time in the main building while you work for me. You'll need to watch that station for anything suspicious. You'll also need to watch those three nurses like a hawk. I don't trust any of them."

"I'll spend a good bit of my time around them," Bess nodded. "Of course, I can't guarantee anything. What if I see nothing out of the ordinary?"

"Then we'll regroup and find a new way to solve this problem," Waynright answered and he leaned forward and poked the top of his desk with his index finger. "It must be solved, Mrs. Bullock. That is the bottom line. Discretion would be my preference but if that doesn't work I'll be more direct in getting to the bottom of this."

"I see," Bess quietly said and she stood up. "Then I'll do what I can."

Mr. Waynright stood up and picked up the receiver to his phone on his desk.

"Let me call to make sure the shuttle is waiting to take you home," Mr. Waynright said, quickly poking at buttons on his phone.

"Thank you," Bess answered before stepping out of the office.

As she walked to the main entrance, where she assumed the shuttle would be waiting, Bess found her curiosity leading her down another hallway. She made an abrupt turn to the right, away from the main entrance, and wandered down another hallway. She took a left and strolled down another hallway. In her mind, she could hear Mr. Waynright speak of the nurses working at that station. Bess was curious to put some faces with the suspects she would be observing.

She turned at yet another corner, one eye still on the familiar room numbers and stopped. There, about ten feet away, she spotted the suspected nurses and the station. She stood at the corner of the hallway and watched the three nurses working there.

One of them was seated and typing on a computer while the other two were reviewing charts. There was nothing terribly unique about them....average looks, slender builds. Two of them were younger, maybe in their twenties. The third one looked older, with glasses and dark curly hair. *Tomorrow*, Bess told herself, *she would watch them more closely. Tomorrow she'd figure out which of them was the culprit.*

Chapter 33: UNDER SUSPICION

The next day, Bess kissed Chet goodbye, reminded
him to take an aspirin for the pain in his back, and then
headed down Dogwood Lane on her way to the main
building. Mr. Waynright had called in the morning to
see if Bess wanted him to send a shuttle for her but the
blue sky and the warm sunshine lured her into walking.
It was a walk that found her mind less appreciative of
the autumnal scenery. Her pace was quicker and
deliberate. Her mind was focused on the task at hand. It
felt good to keep busy rather than sitting around the
house thinking about her brother.

When she reached the main building, Bess glanced
at the map Mr. Waynright had given her and she made
her way to the station that she was supposed to spy on.
Along the way, she began to recognize the room
numbers she was passing. They matched the room
numbers from the map.

So these are the people in pain, Bess told herself.

She was interested in seeing some faces of the
victims who were affected by this theft of pain pills.
Bess lingered by some of the rooms. The doors were
open a bit, so she peeked inside at each of the residents.

She spotted one room that contained a resident who
was wheelchair bound. One room had a very thin
woman adjusting her sweater while looking out her
window. Another room found a woman seated in a
chair reading a newspaper with a magnifying glass.
Bess also noticed that this woman had a walker close
by. Yet another room featured a man watching TV with
a walking cane next to his chair. It was clear to Bess

that these were residents who were in various forms of pain from day to day. These were residents who were being affected by someone taking their pain pills.

Bess moved down the hallway back to the station she was to watch. There she saw the nurses beginning their shift. It was the two younger nurses and the older nurse—the same faces Bess had seen yesterday. All three were working in tandem, organizing papers and adjusting meds for the beginning of their shift. What drew Bess's attention was the older nurse who was dispensing meds into small plastic cups for residents to take. There was no question it was tedious work, but it was work that had to be done. Suddenly, the nurse dispensing the medicine looked up and made eye contact with Bess.

"I know who you are," the nurse said, her eyes shifting back to the cups she was filling with pills. "You're Bess Bullock. I remember when you lived in this building. I was the nurse who used to give you your meds. You were always one of the more interesting residents to talk to."

The older nurse smiled after her comment and Bess's eyes quickly took in the details—her spiked blond hair, her blue eyes, her tan skin that looked more leathery than smooth.

"Your name was…Greta?" Bess said, recalling the fact that when she lived in the main building she was served a mid-morning snack and a mid-afternoon snack by Nurse Greta.

"I'm impressed," Greta replied. "It's been almost two years, Mrs. Bullock. I must have made quite an impression on you."

"You were kind to my granddaughter when she visited," Bess replied. "You always brought extra graham crackers for Nicole and me when she came by. That's the kind of gesture one doesn't forget."

"Do you remember when you talked to me about your work as a police officer?" Greta said and she slipped a piece of gum in her mouth and began to chew it nervously. "You had many good stories to tell me back then. I remember how you started to uncover some mischief around here, too. You took such pleasure in telling me stories about the mysteries you'd find. Are you still looking for mysteries?"

"On occasion," Bess nodded.

The comment drew a steely gaze from Greta's blue eyes. She pressed her lips together and grabbed some papers off a nearby desk.

"Well, Mrs. Bullock, you won't find anything like that here!" Greta remarked with a sharper tone in her voice.

Bess was surprised by Greta's comment. Bess could only guess that, unlike the younger nurses, Greta had a clue as to what was going on.

"Really," Bess replied and she smiled. "Thank you for the tip, but I'm not looking for a mystery today. I'm here to visit a friend."

"I'm sorry," Greta replied as she scribbled her name on some papers. "It's just that I have a lot on my mind and when I saw you pop up here, I just thought…never mind. I apologize for snapping at you."

"So is there something curious upsetting you?" Bess hinted. "Something about your job that's making you short with residents like me?"

"I have a teenage son at home," Greta stated and a slight grin pushed across her face. "If you've ever raised a teenager, you know that can put you on edge. Sometimes it's hard to leave that tension at home."

"I'm a mother," Bess nodded. "I do remember those stressful years with my daughter."

"That's really all I can say," Greta replied. She paused, looked around, and then leaned in closer to

Bess. "If you were looking for a mystery to solve, Mrs. Bullock, I'm afraid there's nothing here for you to find. It's simply me and these nice young nurses doing our jobs. We're all honest. We all need to provide for our families. If someone asked you to come here today…you can tell them what I said."

"That's good to know," Bess began and she took one step away from the counter. She gestured to a chair and began to walk towards it. "I'm going to sit here for a while and wait for my friend. It's nice to know that you and the other nurses are such good people."

For the next hour, Bess remained seated, glancing over at the activity of the nurses from time to time. On occasion, her eyes met Nurse Greta's eyes by accident, which led to uncomfortable smiles from both ladies. Bess had a sense that Greta knew why she was there. Yet, despite Greta's suspicions, Bess refused to leave. If, as Greta asserted, no wrongs were being committed, then Bess felt more entitled to continue her observation.

At one point, Greta disappeared down a hallway, pushing a cart that Bess quickly recognized as a snack cart. It was the same kind of cart that Greta used to serve crackers and juice to Bess years earlier when she lived in the main building. Bess quickly reasoned that Greta would be gone for a while, knowing how many rooms she had to serve.

With this assumption fresh in her thoughts, Bess decided to stand up and wander a little closer to the station to get a better view of the younger nurses in action. She quickly spotted one young nurse attending to a tray of cups. Next to the tray were a variety of pill containers. The nurse checked the list, dumped pills into a cup, and then marked the cup with the name of the person for whom the medicine was intended.

"My goodness, look at all those pills," Bess sighed.

"People need their pills, darling," the younger nurse spoke up while she continued to mark the cups with names of residents.

"Lots of people around here do," Bess observed.

"Yes, and they need them every day," the nurse nodded.

"I take oxycodone," Bess fibbed and she grimaced and pointed down to one leg. "A touch of arthritis in my knee."

"Well, then, this bottle would be for you," the young nurse said and she dangled a large baby blue bottle in the air. Bess noted that the other bottles were orange or clear. There was only one bottle that was blue. Bess guessed it was designated that way to make it easier for nurses to find. Whatever the explanation, Bess knew the distinguishing color of the bottle would now make it easier for her to keep one eye on the oxycodone.

"I guess you're lucky if you don't need pills," Bess smiled.

The comment did not elicit any response from the nurse. Over the years Bess found all the nurses to be very kind and courteous, but professional. There was a fine line between outright friendliness and keeping emotions under control to do a job. The nurses at the Honey Hills Center tended to keep their emotions in check. They were polite. They smiled when needed. However, Bess could tell the feelings weren't from the heart. Like the people she rode in business class with on the train, the nurses were professional to a fault.

When the last of the medicine was dispensed, Bess watched the young nurse collect all the pill containers and carry them behind the counter. Bess walked around the counter to continue to make eye contact with the containers. She was surprised that the younger nurse didn't say anything at Bess's overt snooping. She watched the nurse tuck the containers in a cabinet and walk away. It appeared to Bess that all the medicine was kept in that cabinet. She looked around and found a seat that allowed her to view the cabinet from a distance.

Now I wait, Bess told herself.

As the hours went by, the nurses continued to flutter in and out of their station. Bess could only liken it to the way hummingbirds dance around a blossom. The nurses kept themselves quite busy in and around their station, but not one of them approached the cabinet that contained the medicine. Soon Bess could feel her stomach growl and she began to realize that, in getting swept up in her observations, she had accidently skipped her lunch.

"Excuse me," Bess said, walking over to one of the nurses seated at a desk. "Do you have any juice or crackers?"

"It's lunch time, sweetie," the young nurse advised with the kind of tone of voice that reminded Bess of her elementary school teacher. "You might want to go eat."

"I will," Bess quickly countered. "I'm drinking more juice to keep my vitamin C up. You see, some people in my hallway have a cold and I don't want to catch it."

The young nurse stared at Bess for a moment, looking at her like she'd just requested a large pizza to eat. Bess knew that every station had a refrigerator that nurses could access for storing medicine and juice containers.

"Let me see what we have here," she finally replied.

Bess stood patiently at the counter, watching the younger nurses and Greta circulate around the station. One young nurse was on the phone. Greta was signing papers at her desk. Then a young nurse returned with a small sealed cup of orange juice.

"Here you go, dear," she grinned, handing it to Bess.

"Thank you," Bess said.

The very second the cup left the nurse's hand, Bess focused on the expression on the nurse's face. She noticed how the warm expression vanished the second Bess pulled the cup from her fingers. *Yet another example,* Bess thought, *that sincerity didn't run deep with nurses.*

She gulped down the cup of cold juice hoping it would cut her appetite. She felt recharged and resumed her watch over the cabinet and the meds well into the afternoon. Bess was grateful that she was at an age where she didn't need to eat as much as she did years earlier. At her age, a full breakfast took her mind off lunch, as was the case today.

After pacing around the nurses station, she found a table not far from the station. It contained some pieces to an unfinished jigsaw puzzle that was spread across the top of the table. Bess quickly sat down and began to work on the puzzle.

Every few seconds, she'd see movement out of the corner of her eye and she'd glance over to the nurses. She had a clear view of the station and the cabinet that contained the medicine. On one occasion, Bess saw a young nurse go for the cabinet and pull out a small orange bottle and place the pill in a plastic cup.

Through the morning and well into the afternoon, Bess continued to keep one eye on the nurses moving in and out of their station. In between glances, she'd work on the puzzle, talk to fellow residents who stopped by, and even had one resident join her in working on the puzzle. Every so often, her eyes turned back to the nurses. She'd spent the better part of her day watching them, but it appeared that none of the nurses had any reason to pull up a blue pill bottle containing oxycodone. None of the nurses even removed the blue bottle from the cabinet. On occasion, Greta would pass by and glance over at Bess with a knowing smile. At one point, she even walked over to where Bess was sitting and whispered,

"I told you there's no mystery here."

Soon it was getting close to dinner time. Bess saw some new nurses begin to filter in for the next shift. She had spent all of her morning and the better part of the afternoon observing three hard-working nurses. She watched the younger nurses huddle with the incoming nurses, showing them papers they were documenting and making conversation about patients. Bess spotted Greta pulling out the tray with the medicine containers on it and she began to fill paper cups for another round of doses.

Bess stepped closer to the counter, aware of not being too obvious but getting a clear view of what was happening. Nurse Greta removed a variety of containers, including the blue container with the oxycodone, and began to fill certain cups with the medication for the evening.

As she watched Nurse Greta organize the medicine, Bess saw something curious appear behind the nurse's station. It was a young man, maybe high-school aged, stepping around the corner with a knowing grin on his face. Bess watched him sneak up behind Greta and give her a quick hug and a kiss on the cheek. Greta smiled and turned around to see the boy. She checked her watch, nodded quickly to the boy and put the bottles of medicine back in the cabinet.

"The teenager," Bess whispered to herself. "So that's your son."

It was in that moment, that brief moment right after she said those words, that Bess saw something remarkable. The young man, in a couple of seconds, dropped a small white pill into a cup and removed another pill while Greta's back was turned. He tucked the pill into his pants pocket and then smiled as Greta collected her things to leave.

Suddenly, Bess had a sense for what was going on. Now she knew why Greta was so strong in her belief that she and the other nurses were doing nothing wrong. Now she realized why the nurses never tested positive from a drug test. She even thought of the police officer, and how the officer who tried to investigate was probably so focused on the nurses that the thought of considering the son of a nurse was never imagined. The son, in turn, probably heard about the officer from his mother. The son probably refrained from taking any pills until the police officer was no longer around. Bess could feel a rush of thoughts filling her head and when the rush was complete, all of her thoughts boiled down to three simple words.

"Such a shame," Bess sighed to herself.

With those words, she walked by the nursing station one last time.

"Greta," Bess smiled and she pointed to the young man standing behind the counter. "Who is this handsome young man?"

"This is my son," Greta answered with a smile that Bess did not recognize. *Perhaps*, Bess told herself, *it was because for the first time all day she'd just seen Greta express a sincere expression of happiness.*

"Is he here to surprise you?" Bess asked.

"He's picking me up," Greta replied. "We've had one car in the shop for about a month, so he's been bringing me to work and picking me up."

"I see," Bess smiled. "Well, it was nice to meet you."

The young man offered a quick smile, then walked away with his mother. Bess watched them move down the hallway, mother just ahead of the son, and she knew what she was going to report. She also knew, it wouldn't be pleasant for Greta to hear.

Chapter 34: SUSPICIONS AT SUNSET

After dinner, Bess and Chet went out on their back porch, settled into their favorite chairs, and let the details of the evening envelope them like a comfortable quilt. There were hints of cricket calls filling the yard. A bird slipped down from the auburn sky before coming to rest in a nearby tree. Cotton candy clouds gently moved across the sky, changing from golden to red to violet. No matter how many times she and Chet sat in their chairs to reflect on the day, the beauty of the evening never ceased to render them both silent.

"I feel like I got cheated out of this day," Bess sighed, her eyes taking in every detail. "I spent too much time in that main building watching those nurses."

"Yes," Chet said, and he looked at her. "You were gone for a long time today, Bess. I was beginning to feel like a widower."

"I'm sorry, dear," Bess sighed.

"I understand," Chet said. "How did the president of the Honey Hills Center react to your discovery?"

"Of course, Mr. Waynright was going to contact the police with what I found," Bess began. "He checked some security tapes to verify what I saw...a very discreet man indeed. Naturally, he was relieved to learn that one of his nurses wasn't stealing pain pills," Bess began.

"I could only imagine the headlines in the newspapers," Chet nodded.

"News like that wouldn't be good for business," Bess agreed. "I would imagine it will be a much easier problem to resolve having the son of that nurse to implicate."

"Yes," Chet smiled. "Job well done, my love. We should celebrate."

Bess nodded to Chet, then shifted her eyes up to the sky and grew silent. The expression on her face no longer appeared happy or pleased with the topic of their conversation.

"What's the matter?' Chet asked. "You don't look happy with yourself."

"It's the mother in me, Chet," Bess said. "I feel for that nurse…Greta. It makes any mother sad when their child makes bad choices. I'm hopeful that Greta will find it in her heart to forgive him. Samantha was quite a handful in high school, and I'll be the first to admit that I lost my patience more than once raising her."

"I had all boys," Chet mumbled and he squinted up to the sky like he was looking at their faces. "A daughter sounds too demanding to me."

"You have no idea," Bess laughed. She reached over, took Chet's hand and smiled.

Silence settled into the air between them. Their eyes were drawn to the scarlet colored sky and the deep violet clouds that clung to the horizon. The sounds of crickets were more pronounced. The evening light was dying. A hush fell between Bess and the world. Peace had settled in her yard, her garden and her heart.

Chapter 35: A PRESENCE IN THE DARK

Most evenings, Bess enjoyed sitting on her back porch staring at the sunset and reflecting on her day. She'd sit with Chet, thinking back on the small achievements that filled their morning and afternoon. Sometimes the colors of the sky even helped her mind to relax and consider the many possibilities of whatever little mysteries she was looking into. However, on this particular evening there were no mysteries to ponder. For the first time in weeks, she could finally look at a sunset and simply appreciate its beauty that filled the skies over her neighborhood.

On this warm evening in October, the Pumpkin Parade was officially underway. Residents of the Honey Hills Retirement Community filled the streets to see the various pumpkins on display. Samantha and Nicole came over to join Chet and Bess in checking out some of the pumpkins on display on her neighbor's porches. Together they walked around the grounds of Honey Hills, moving from one front porch to the next.

Along the way, Bess spotted Audrey and Eveline Green walking down Dogwood Lane. Bess smiled at the sight of mother and daughter together again. A little while later, she spotted Buster and Marty walking down the street. Buster proudly clutched his leash in his mouth while Marty smiled lovingly at her new dog in training. Even Alma and her fiancé, Paul Ford, were strolling hand in hand, pointing at the various pumpkins. Bess smiled at the love that clearly filled the air around them, and briefly thought about how hard it would be to refer to Alma as Mrs. Ford.

While she walked and continued along the Pumpkin Parade route, Bess glanced down at Nicole and smiled when she saw her granddaughter slip her hand into Chet's hand. Bess could feel her heart flutter at the sight of her husband pointing out a pumpkin to Nicole. They both laughed at the pumpkin, which was decorated like a dog. As she did on every front porch, Nicole gave her vote of thumbs up or thumbs down to the pumpkin.

Bess marveled at the many original ideas that her fellow residents had thought of in decorating their pumpkins. She spotted a George Washington pumpkin wearing a white wig, a patriotic hat, and two small flags that poked out the top. On another porch, Nicole became quite fond of a pumpkin that was crafted to look like a cat. Nicole giggled and rushed up to the pumpkin, stating to no one in particular that she thought it resembled the cat she'd seen on the train.

As the evening wore on, the sky took on a darker hue of purple and the air slipped into a subtler degree of coolness. With the twilight fading, some residents began to light their jack-o-lanterns. The golden glow from the pumpkins gave some porches a magical element to the evening.

"This is so beautiful," Samantha sighed. "A perfect evening for this parade of pumpkins, don't you think so, Mother?"

"It is quite lovely," Bess sighed and her eyes turned to her granddaughter. "What do you think, Nicole?"

"I think everything is pretty," Nicole beamed.

Together Bess, Chet, Samantha and Nicole continued to wander the streets of the Honey Hills grounds, finding one pumpkin after another to look at. With the sky turning a deeper hue of purple, Bess noted that the beauty of the evening had not been lost on Samantha. Her trusted cell phone did not make one appearance during their walk. A smile filled her face for most of the evening. At one point, she even took Bess's hand the way she did as a school girl.

"I'm glad you're here," Bess whispered and she gave Samantha's hand a playful squeeze.

Samantha smiled.

"Look at that one!" Nicole called out before running off to investigate another glowing pumpkin. She pulled Chet along with her to investigate.

"Are you coming, Mother?" Samantha asked, stepping after Nicole.

"I'll wait here," Bess smiled. "Go ahead. Catch up to Nicole and Chet."

Bess smiled as she watched Chet, Samantha and Nicole step up to the porch. She stood in the street, then looked up to the sky and her curiosity grew. There was something familiar about this sunset. It was in the shape of the clouds and the way they hung along the horizon, and how the light illuminated them with gold. It all looked strangely familiar to her.

The lavender sky with unusually shaped golden clouds reminded her of an identical sunset she'd seen in California. It was the day of the funeral, when she stepped out of her brother's house and stood on the beach to think back on the events of the day. She could clearly recall staring at the same sky. She was alone on the beach, looking at the sky and thinking of how many times her brother had stared at a similar sunset. How many times had he whispered his wishes to the sky and pondered what the next day would bring for him?

Bess closed her eyes and listened to the laughter of Nicole. She could hear the warm words being spoken between Samantha and Chet. Then she began to sense another presence. It was a presence that she could feel close by. She opened her eyes, looked around at the beauty of the moment: the glowing pumpkins, the violet sky, and the sight of Nicole, Samantha and Chet standing on a porch to study a pumpkin.

She closed her eyes again and could feel the presence return. She could feel that presence in her heart. It was a presence that warmed her heart with emotions she hadn't felt since the funeral. In a matter of seconds, she could sense that the guilt in her heart was beginning to fade. She could only liken it to how the morning fog lifts when rays of bright light fill in dark places.

She opened her eyes and looked up at the rich colors that filled the horizon. She placed her hand on her chest and smiled. Of all the suspicions she had pondered at sunset, the mystery of her vanishing guilt did not require her to think of a solution. She didn't need facts to explain how she felt. Instead, she chose to let her faith be the reason. Faith and the smile on her face, were the only things she needed to tell her that her guilt, for the first time in weeks, had subsided.

Chapter 36: TIME TO DANCE

By all accounts, the Pumpkin Parade was a tremendous success. As the days went by, Bess heard many conversations from residents about the Pumpkin Parade. Bess often recalled to Chet some of the creative pumpkins they'd seen on display. Chet reflected on the many reasons why he thought his clown pumpkin didn't win. They both agreed it was nice to do something different. The Pumpkin Parade was a nice way to break up the day-to-day routines that they followed in a retirement community.

However, the routine of life soon returned, the way the ocean always finds a way back to the shore. The weekly routine of meetings, medical appointments, and morning walks filled each day again. After weeks of mourning her brother's death, Bess found it nice to have a familiar routine to settle into. She also learned that keeping busy with investigating little mysteries was also good for coping with her grief. Yet, not all of her old routine had been restored.

Ever since she first became a resident of the Honey Hills Center, Bess and Chet were members of the Waltzing Club. Over the years they'd grown accustomed to dancing with each other once a week. For as long as she'd known Chet, he'd always been the president of the Waltzing Club. It was Chet who always coordinated the music and dance moves for the club. He still followed through with these responsibilities as president, even though he was still unable to participate.

Since his sciatic nerve had flared up, he'd been homebound for the better part of two months. When Bess first returned from California, she was consumed by her grief. As time went by, she began to see that Chet's bad back and inactivity were wearing on him. *After all,* she thought, *there were only so many newspapers to read and crossword puzzles to do.*

Every morning over breakfast, Chet would give her an update on his condition. While there was some improvement during his lengthy break from dancing, his back wasn't improving as quickly as he wanted. Chet normally was an upbeat person. Bess began to notice that being unable to dance was wearing down his optimistic nature. One evening, Bess decided to do something about it.

After dinner, it was Chet's turn to wash the dirty dishes. While he worked, Bess carried a small radio into the living room, turned on some soft jazz music, and sat on the couch and waited for Chet to finish cleaning up. When Chet emerged from the kitchen, Bess turned up the music on the radio, stood up and walked over to him. She gently took his hand with her fingers and smiled.

"Dance with me," she whispered.

"I can't," Chet replied. "The doctor said I shouldn't."

"The doctors don't know you like I do," Bess softly spoke. "I didn't notice it when I first got back from California, but I can tell you miss it."

"I know," Chet mumbled. "I miss dancing with you, Twinkle Toes. Sometimes I think I'll never have a day without pain in my back and legs. You know how it is as we get old, Bess. Our bodies change for the worse and there's never a guarantee that the pain you feel one day will go away or not. Maybe I'll just have to live with this pain for the rest of my life. That's something I've been thinking about more and more."

Bess reached over and gently brushed his full white hair to the side.

"I'm sorry, Chet," Bess said.

"For what?" Chet asked.

"I feel like I've spent so many days focusing my thoughts on the dead, that I've neglected you. You've been right here, Chet...and I feel like I've ignored you. All this time you've been hobbled by this pinched nerve in your back and I've ignored it. All this time you've been unable to dance, and I've ignored it. I've just been too preoccupied with my grief to notice how much it has been bothering you."

Chet smiled and shook his head just a little.

"It sounds like we both have had our share of worries," Chet sighed.

"Do you know what I love most about dancing with you?" Bess asked.

"Tell me," Chet said.

"Getting lost on the dance floor," Bess stated. "I remember how the music would fill my ears. I remember how you'd fill my eyes. When I'd step on the dance floor with you, all my worries would disappear. Take my hand, Chet, and dance with me."

"I don't know if I can," Chet answered and he looked down at the floor.

"It's okay," Bess pointed out and she reached over and gently placed her hand on his cheek. "The music is slow. Just take my hand, hold me, and let's move together. If we're careful, I think you'll be okay. Let's try it. Let's see if we can dance, get lost in the music and forget our troubles for a little while."

Chet nodded and his bright blue eyes turned up and centered on Bess. His large hand wrapped around her waist. His other hand, warm and soft, gently wrapped around her hand. He stepped close to her. She felt her heart flutter as she looked into his sky blue eyes. He smiled.

With the evening sky beginning to unfurl bouquets of pink and gold in their picture window, they carefully moved around the living room. Their steps were measured. Their eyes never left each other. The sound of a trumpet playing a sad song dripped from the air. She gripped his hand. She smiled and he smiled back. She closed her eyes and placed her head against his chest. Her toes tingled. She closed her eyes. Her worries were gone.

ABOUT THE AUTHOR

 Allen B. Boyer is the author of two Young Adult novels and one nonfiction book about the West Point Academy and its famous graduates. His books have been sold around the country. This is his fifth cozy mystery. The first, *Gumshoe Granny Investigates,* introduced Bess Bullock, the protagonist of the Bess Bullock Retirement Home Mystery series. The second, *Clues Over Croissants*, followed Bess on further adventures. In the third book, *Married to Mysteries*, Bess marries her dancing partner Chet Wooden and finds that marriage forces certain adjustments to her detecting style. In the fourth book, *Whispers in Winter,* Bess continues her sleuthing as a married woman.

Mr. Boyer lives near Hershey, Pennsylvania, with his wife, Suzanne, and their three children. He likes to take his children and their dog to visit residents at a nearby retirement home.

www.ingramcontent.com/pod-product-compliance
Lightning Source LLC
Chambersburg PA
CBHW020326260626

47156CB00004B/1392